NAVIGATING RUINS

WRITING THE FUTURE WE NEED

HOLLY SCHOFIELD   TIM KANE   ANNA ZIEGELHOF

LAMONT A. TURNER   CALLUM ROWLAND

GREGORY J. GLANZ   A'LIYA SPINNER

ISABEL HUNTOON   A.J. VAN BELLE

WriteHive is a nonprofit providing **FREE** inclusive events, programming, and resources for writers of all backgrounds. Get notified of our upcoming events and programs by signing up to our newsletter or checking out our website!

This anthology, as well as everything we do, is funded 100% by volunteers and your donations—and now through revenue from the sale of this anthology.

Thank you for giving this book a read! We hope you enjoy the stories. If you are able, we would be grateful if you wrote a review on Amazon, Goodreads, or Indie Story Geek.

Kindest Regards,
    The WriteHive Team

FOREWORD

Readers,

We are in an era of change. At the start of this decade, we entered a global pandemic and faced multiple trying situations that made us take a hard look at our lives and values. Entering 2021, it felt like many things were shattered—ideas, lives, families, politics, all of it left in ruins, with some pieces more intact than others. Now, we are navigating the ruins of what happened and what was exposed during that time.

The stories within this anthology explore what it means to navigate those ruins. It's different for everyone. Each story is a different take, a different way to explore these facets. Sometimes you can only sit within the ruins and mourn the loss of what was. Other times there's fear of what may come. For others, there's hope for new beginnings.

"Writing the Future We Need" will always be a part of our anthologies. Words have power, and together we can shape a better, brighter world, one in which the voice of hate is silenced. We'll work toward that future, no matter how long it takes.

We hope you enjoy the stories we have for you. If you like what you've read, please consider leaving us a review.

Bee the Change,

Jerusha René (She/Her)
     WriteHive CEO

WHAT YOU SOW
HOLLY SCHOFIELD

Trigger Warning: Terminal illness

Your earliest memory is of your mother's brush as she yanks it through the tangle of Kentucky bluegrass carpeting your head. She clicks her tongue and plucks a few dandelion sprouts. You wince and she murmurs comfort.

You hold that memory close after every argument. The time when you are eight years old and try to tuck snowdrop bulbs behind your ears, thinking she won't notice until it's time to trim the turf edge that hovers over your eyebrows. The time when you are twelve, and you defiantly plant scarlet zinnias, arched across your head like a tiara, a weak imitation of the coolest kids at school. She lets you get away with it for a whole month then knocks on your bedroom door, pruning shears in hand.

You begin to collect picture books of ornate headgardens. Your usual answer to adults asking what you want to be when you grow up becomes "hortulist," and your mother rolls her eyes every time. Once, you stop in the street, yank on your mother's sleeve, and stare at a man with tiny leafy evergreens scattered across his head, roots clinging in fibrous knots. "Sequoia. *So* cool!" you breathe, eyes wide.

Your mother's tongue clicks. "Waste of money. Just think about how heavy they'll be in a few years, how many calories that will require." Your mother speaks too loudly, patting her own never-changing English daisies, the petite kind with very short stems. They carpet her scalp like an old-fashioned swim cap.

At fifteen, you let weeds sprout and grow until they smother your ears and trail over the curve of your back, dried bits snarling up in the living room carpet and littering your sweaters. You slam your bedroom door whenever your mother comments.

As summer wanes, spiny weed seeds fall inside your shirt collar and you spend a year's allowance at the hortulist's the day before school starts. The pampas grasses take many minutes of styling in the mirror each morning; the plumes need to be just the right amount of feathery before you can leave the house. You grow used to your mother pounding on the bathroom door.

By spring you are dating a classmate, their head shaggy with deep-green moss, their neck rife with the damp scent of forests and the snubbing of tradition. You ask them to wear a graduation mortarboard in their yearbook photo, which you think would look nice since it would cover all but a fringe of their sphagnum. After they dump you, you wonder if that thought had been your mother's and not your own.

In your final year of high school, you become politically aware—at least you think you do—and you replace the pampas with Swiss chard. You harvest it every week to donate to the homeless shelter, but you become weary of strangers plucking at your head when you stand in line at the mall. After a crowd of boys tease you about how tasty you look, you chop it all off and plant the cheapest and most popular mix—blue-bonnets and poppies and cornflowers—and refuse to discuss it with your mother.

The flower mixture ends when you get your first job. You hate your new corporate look of sleek, over-fertilized lawn but love the paychecks. You learn to keep your tongue motionless at the clear double standard in the office: under your boss's tweed cap lies unkempt yellowed bent-grass.

When you make infrequent visits home, your mother's sidelong glances accompany the style magazines placed prominently on the coffee table.

Over time, your mother's English daisies become withered and brown. There are other symptoms: stomach pains and weight loss. She enters the hospital and you visit every day.

You brush crumpled leaves off her pillow while the doctors mutter about end-of-life stages and palliative care options.

After the funeral, you march into the most expensive hortulist in the city. The wildflowers you purchase then will hug your head for many years to come.

Now, they dangle above your newborn's face. You hold your baby tightly, inhaling the milk scent of her unsown head, and you whisper promises into tiny ears, as your native oxeye daisies swing free and untamed.

HOLLY SCHOFIELD

Holly Schofield's stories have appeared in Lightspeed, Analog, Escape Pod, and many other publications throughout the world. You can find her at hollyschofield.wordpress.com.

WOLF IN SHEEP'S CLOTHING
CLOTHING

TIM KANE

Trigger Warning: Degenerative Illness, Suicide

iny tumbleweeds of dust clutter the hardwood floor. I peer at the seams where the boards connect. This is how it creeps into the house—bit by bit. The sun is setting and the opened curtains only let in a little light. Is that a strand of white hiding beneath the grime? I hold the spray bottle close, finger on the trigger. Have to be sure. Don't want to waste the bleach.

"Elsie!" Conrad calls from the couch. "What's a footman?"

I don't have the energy to answer one of his many questions right now. Glancing over, his mop of hair looks like it got into a scuffle with the vacuum and lost. He squints at the book of fairy tales, knees pulled to his chest. Sometimes I wish he did more than just read Mom's book. I roll my shoulders, trying to loosen the muscles. Everything aches. Princesses get saved all the time in those stories. Where's my happily ever after?

I squeeze the trigger, just so I don't have to stare at this spot anymore. But then I regret it. A swirl of the plastic bottle shows less than an inch of liquid left.

Hazel cries from her basket. It's set on the floor near the window, but not too near. The fading rays of sunlight wash over the makeshift crib, leaving crosshatch shadows from the interwoven wicker handles. She wiggles one pudgy hand above the rim. It might be her diaper. But that can wait.

I scan the baseboards along the wall, the wood patchy from too many hits with the sprayer. A lump in the corner looks suspicious. I squeeze the trigger, but instead of a stream of liquid, the bleach dribbles onto my jeans. *Dammit.* Cinderella only had to deal with soot. My clothes have this brown muck coating nearly every inch. Add in a healthy spattering of white spots from the bleach and it makes me look like a mottled hyena.

I head to the shelves Dad threw together, just some planks

set up on stacked cinder blocks. Bottles of water line the top, but only half are full. The bottom shelf holds the remaining bleach. I reach for the plastic jug too fast and my arm whacks the wood.

"Shit!"

I swivel toward Conrad. He's still curled up on the sagging couch, nose in the book. Good, he didn't hear me. Mom never likes us to curse. Thinks it's improper.

I roll my sleeve back for a peek—the fabric so threadbare it nearly tears. The scrape runs up to the elbow, thin with only a little blood. Not too bad. But when I bend my arm, a sting of pain needles the skin. Got some splinters jammed in there. Not enough light to pull them out now. What a waste. I banged myself up to see something I already knew. A jiggle of the plastic jug tells me it's nearly empty. There's a half-full bottle of ammonia, but that just repels. Bleach is the only thing that kills the stuff.

The ceiling creaks. Is that Mom? Maybe she's feeling better. I can picture the curve of her smile. How the strands of her hair would catch on her lipstick when she laughed. Mom always told us bedtime stories. Even though I'm too old for them, I'd still eavesdrop when she'd read to Conrad or Hazel. She calls us her "Little Piggies" after the Big Bad Wolf story.

I listen again, hoping to hear another creak. Nothing. She must be lying in bed. Mom's been up there three days now.

Hazel cries—a series of sobs building in strength. Something is wrong. Her arms, highlighted red in the setting sun, flail in the air. Conrad sits on the couch still reading Mom's book of fairy tales. He doesn't even notice.

Hazel's crying is sure to be heard outside. I scurry over. Shadows fill up the basket, leaving her a little more than a silhouette. I can't turn on a light. Not with the curtains still open. Is she hungry? There's only one can of formula left and hardly any water. Part of the reason Dad went on the supply run. But he's never been gone this long.

Hazel sees me. Her hands clutch the air, wanting to be lifted up. My muscles stiffen. I peer into the basket, letting my eyes adjust to the shadows. She's scrunched up to one side. What's she getting away from? I lean closer and see them— thin white tendrils grasping for her tiny body. A chill scuttles up my spine. The fungus has infested the whole side of the basket.

"Conrad!"

I scoot the basket with my foot and Hazel lets out a shriek of surprise. A tangle of fungus has burst through the floorboards. Moving the basket severed the tendrils, but even detached, they still twist toward Hazel.

Conrad comes up beside me. When he spots the fungus inching across the floor, he takes a step back.

"Grab the bleach," I say.

He shakes his head. His gaze is still fixated on the Bloom.

I stare at Hazel in her basket. My hands tremble. Why am I hesitating?

White tendrils seize Hazel's leg. She screams.

"Stop it."

I jab my hands in the basket, plucking her up. Hazel squirms in my grip, arms and legs kicking. My chest constricts. I can't hold onto her. She's going to fall. Just like before. I stagger back, feel the world spin around me. She screeches, right in my ear. Sweat dribbles into my eyes, blurring the world. My foot strikes the basket and I stumble. My grip on Hazel slips. I twist and manage to plop her onto the couch cushions.

I collapse on the floor. Tears gush down my face, a storm of sobbing that can't be stopped.

I gaze up at the ceiling, toward Mom. She needs to come

down here and take over. But the house remains silent. No movement from upstairs. The only sound is my blubbering, now trickling down to a whimper.

Conrad stands there, staring at me. Even with the dwindling light, I can see his eyes shot wide—the hyper-focused way they get when he's freaked out. But he'll just have to deal. Hazel comes first. And that means more light.

"Pull the curtains."

He looks at me, confused.

"The curtains." There's still a tremor in my voice, the residue of my mini freak out. "But don't show yourself."

Conrad nods. Having something to do seems to calm him down. He shuffles toward the windows.

I pull out my cell phone. No service. Hasn't been any for weeks. So now it's the world's most expensive flashlight. I smile. How I begged Dad for the newest model, just so I could message my friends. Keep up on social media. What would my update be now?

```
Hey. Just freaked the hell out 'cause
   some fungus tried to eat my little
     sister. Be sure to like my post.
```

My friends are probably dead.

Conrad pulls the curtains across the front window and the house goes dark. I turn on the phone's flashlight. It hardly has any power, so this might be its last use. The beam reflects off Hazel's eyes and she giggles. She's always been quick to recover. Not like Conrad. With him, just stubbing a toe means the world is coming to an end. If he'd been a little more like Hazel, then maybe I'd be able to handle things better.

I shake loose those thoughts. They aren't helping. Hazel looks clear, but then, so did Mom. I lift her pudgy arms, inspecting the skin. Then the legs. When the Bloom infects you, it leaves a red rash. Mom finally found hers on the back of her ankle. But it's not what you see on the outside that matters. The fungus sneaks through your body, straight for the brain. With Mom, it changed the way she thought.

Hazel coos. She thinks me lifting her legs is some sort of game. I grab a few sagging cushions and stuff them around as a sort of makeshift crib. As far as I can tell, she's fine. Not a mark on her.

I start to stand. A wave of dizziness strikes me and I thump back onto the floor. There's something else I need to do, but my thoughts flow like syrup. How long has it been since I ate breakfast? Slurping down that can of cold chicken soup?

I close my eyes, let my body relax. I'll have to get up soon. Get everyone some food. And that means trudging over to the kitchen. But it can wait a moment.

Dad should be back by now.

The worry sticks in my head. I stare at the front door. The knob will turn and it'll be Dad. Back when Mom was still okay, I used to go on some of the runs. Dad and I went only last week. Seems like months ago.

The grocery store had collapsed on one side. The wall just eaten away, leaving only metal struts and piles of nails. Half-opened packages littered the aisles, most from the rush after the first few days of the Bloom. But every time I'd gone with Dad, the place was abandoned. The fungus had totally overrun the produce and meat sections, smothering them with a white blanket of interwoven tendrils. A few of those red flowers scattered along the surface.

I was all bundled up, the way Dad taught me—gloves, masks, goggles. Even duct tape wrapped around my wrists and ankles. That's how it got to Mom. The tape had snagged on a shelf and pulled loose.

We were after the canned food. And more bleach. But I'd come here so many times, it didn't seem like much of a threat. More like an abandoned playground. I'd charge up and down the aisles, my boots smooshing the fungus along the floor. I made it a game: How fast could I nab the cans and bring them to the cart? I wanted to bring back all the ravioli, so I'd pulled my shirt out as a makeshift bag and it exposed my stomach, but only a little. I wasn't thinking about what could happen.

I dashed back to the cart. But Dad glared at me through his goggles.

"I got all the ravioli. Did I do good?" I only wanted to see him smile. He hardly seemed happy anymore.

"Tuck your shirt in." Frustration flashed across his eyes. "This isn't a game."

I dumped the cans in the cart. "There's some beef stew, too." When I spun around to run back, my shoe caught on the lumpy fungus floor. I fell, sprawled out on the aisle. Dad yanked me up so fast, it felt like he pulled my arm out of the socket. He knelt and inspected my stomach. After a moment, he gently tucked my shirt back in.

"You're fourteen now, Elsie. You have to take this seriously."

And because he couldn't trust me, Mom went on the next run. So it's really my fault. If I had just been more responsible, then maybe . . . I glance up at the ceiling. Things would be different.

Conrad shakes me. Why is his face so dark? I look over at the window. Curtains still pulled. But instead of the glow of the sun behind them, there's only blackness. What happened?

"I'm hungry," Conrad says.

"Why did you let me fall asleep?" I push myself up. A wave of dizziness strikes me, and I grip the couch's arm for support. The splinters in my elbow itch terribly.

"You didn't sleep." He points at the door, now a shadowy rectangle. "You just kept looking." He lowers his arm. "I didn't want to bother you."

I switch on the phone. At first the light won't turn on, but after a second, it blares to life. There's Hazel, asleep on the couch. I scan the darkened house.

"Daddy said you're in charge. That means you're the mommy now."

"I'm not Mommy," I snap back.

The beam lands on Hazel's basket. It looks deformed—one side sagging in. Totally devoured. A shard of panic jabs my brain. The Bloom.

I sweep the flashlight across the floor. The patch of white fungus has grown. The breach had been near the window, maybe twenty feet from the couch. Now the tendrils creep toward us, only inches from where my legs were.

"Shit."

Conrad sees the fungus and scrambles onto the couch. "Don't let it get me."

I circle around the tendrils, keeping the flashlight trained on them the whole time, and snatch up the spray bottle. One pull of the trigger and I remember. Nearly empty. I unscrew the top and fling the bleach out at the spreading fungus. I don't want to get close enough to do a better job, so half of it over-shoots and spatters the hardwood floor. But where it hits, the tendrils shrivel and turn black.

The whole mass reacts. Instead of slinking toward the couch, the fungus juts out in every direction, trying to escape the bleach. So damn fast.

For an instant I simply stand there as the tendrils slither toward me. It's never been so quick before.

The shelf with the remaining bleach is across the room, but the spreading fungus blocks my way. I leap to an empty spot on the floor and a woozy sensation fills my head. My body teeters, arms pinwheeling to keep my balance. I won't fall. I won't let it win.

Two more jerky steps and I'm at the wall, collapsing against it for support.

Swinging the phone's light back highlights the tendrils as they twist to follow me. How do they know where I am?

I nab the jug, unscrew the cap.

"Hurry," Conrad yells. He's propped up on the couch with Hazel. The fungus wriggles closer to them. Now only a foot away.

No time to fill the sprayer. I slosh the jug forward, splashing the floor with bleach. The tendrils wither. I splatter the whole floor. Left, right, everywhere. It gets on the couch and the half-devoured basket. Probably even the walls. When it's over, I know two things.

I know the room's clear. I scoured every section of floor. Even under the shelves and couch.

And I know I'm out of bleach. The jug is empty. Not even a drop remains.

A tightness wraps around my chest—like being smothered —every breath pushing back an ocean of weight. I glare at the door. Where are you, Dad?

I grab the rubber gloves off the shelf. As I pull them on, my body shudders. I want to cry. Just plop down and let it all go. But there's no one else here. Just me.

I lift Hazel's basket. One side feels squishy and rotten. Bleach trickles out and puddles on the ground. Can't use the flashlight and carry at the same time, so this chore happens in the dark. Even with the dousing the basket took, the fungus can hide in the crevices where the wicker overlaps, which means it isn't safe. I lumber toward the front door, holding the basket away from my body. The less I touch, the less the fungus can spread. Even in the gloom, I make out Hazel's favorite blanket. A pang of anger jabs my chest. Why does the Bloom have to take so much? Everything we care about, destroyed.

I must set the basket down to unlock the door. Conrad sits on the couch, arms wrapped around his legs, watching.

I pull my shirt up over my mouth and open the door. A new landscape covers the neighborhood. Sheets of fungus reflect the pale moonlight, turning their red flowers black. Even through my shirt, the air smells dank and wet, like fresh-turned soil. Everything here used to be normal—two-story townhomes, grass lawns, driveways clogged with cars. Now the houses across the street sag, ready to collapse. The Bloom will get to our house sooner or later. I think of the empty jug of bleach. Maybe sooner.

I toss the basket out, and it topples down the steps, collapsing into a heap. Hazel's basket had seemed so strong. But once infected with the fungus, it crumbled away. I shut the door and lock it.

The Bloom was supposed to solve all our problems, fix global warming by gobbling up all the extra carbon emissions. No more fretting about your carbon footprint. I let out a chuckle. Boy were they wrong. I pull the curtain a little and stare out at what used to be our neighborhood. The Bloom was too good at its job. It devoured any carbon it could find—wood, plastic, clothing. And the super fungus has a special fondness for living things. Easier to digest maybe. The world's best pesticide.

Thin tendrils cling to the other side of the glass. I watch as the fungus creeps along the window. It can move fast when it wants to, but the wooden beams of the house aren't its favorite food. Movement catches my eye. The silhouette of a person, staggering through the street. Hope blossoms in my chest, and

I catch myself smiling. *Dad.* But then I see how the figure stumbles along, arms hanging limp at his sides. Plus this person is too short. Just another rotter. I linger at the window. Maybe I can catch a glimpse of the face. The only time I really saw one up close was six months ago when everything started. That'd been a woman, and the milky white tendrils had exploded from her cheeks and nose and eyes like sea anemone, wriggling and clutching.

The shambling figure veers toward our house. I see its face —sagging and putrid under the moonlight, the features nearly gone, only the whites of his eyes looking out. Staring. A spike of fear. It spotted me. I duck down. Will it rush the house, banging on the door or windows to get in? It's the rotter's only goal, to infect other people. The fungus inside needs to feed.

I wait.

The only sound is the creaking of the house. I glance up at the ceiling. Mom never became one of those things. Never tried to come for us. She fights against the Bloom.

I pull the curtain a sliver, peeking outside. The street looks clear. It must have passed us by. But there's always more.

Turning toward the couch, I see a pale blue glow coming from Conrad's lap. He's got Mom's fairytale book propped up on his knees, and the light radiates up onto his face. What's he using? The glow winks out and Conrad fidgets with something in his lap. I spy the flash of a blue screen and glowing numbers. It's his alarm clock. He keeps pressing the snooze button to get it to light up.

I catch myself smiling. Our little piggie has figured out how to read in the dark. Mom always said Conrad was the clever one.

The fairytale book is nearly falling apart. I don't know what he'd do without it. Now that Mom's locked upstairs, it's become his security blanket. Most of the damage came from the last time Mom read to us. No one knew she was infected. Not even Dad. But the Bloom had worked its way inside her head. She'd space out, sometimes forgetting what she'd just read. Conrad was always there to point out the last part, tapping the page where the wolf dressed up like the grandmother and hid in bed.

Mom used to say that the same wolf moved from story to story. Sometimes he'd go after Little Red Riding Hood, and other times he'd slip on a sheep's skin to nab some lambs. But he was always sneaky. Mom would wiggle her fingers and tickle Conrad, calling him her clever piggie. If I was near enough, she'd get me too, her nails digging into my side. But I'd giggle all the same.

The last time Mom read, everything changed. She got more and more irritated each time Conrad corrected her. Finally, she snapped the book shut and hurled it across the room. "You read it!" Conrad started bawling. Mom seemed to come back to herself and hugged him. It was after the book throwing that she retreated to the bedroom. She had Dad attach a lock to the outside of her door.

"Elsie!"

I blink and see Conrad standing next to me, his face etched with worry. A shadow stretches out behind him. Light streams around the sides of the curtain. What happened? It was just night.

"I'm really hungry," Conrad says. "But I can't open the cans."

Behind us, two dented cans sit on the coffee table. All of the ravioli I'd gotten from the store.

"Elsie?" He grabs my elbow, the one with the splinters. Pain rockets through my arm. I lash out, knocking Conrad back. He whacks his head against the coffee table. Hazel erupts in a bout of cries, arms and legs flailing.

A powerful urge overwhelms me—smash everything. Just reduce the house to rubble. I squeeze my fists so hard my arms quiver. Why am I feeling this way?

Conrad is sobbing. When he turns around, an ugly scrape mars his forehead. A memory flashes through my mind, back when Conrad was only a baby. Of me carrying him to the changing table. Mom was upstairs and Dad was in the garage. I'd just wanted to help. But he was so heavy and squirming all the time. I'd gotten him up onto the changing table and went to grab a fresh diaper. I turned away, only for a second. But that was all it took. Conrad rolled off the table and hit the floor. His wailing filled the whole house. Dad was the first one there. He'd chewed me out about responsibility, and I just stood there. Frozen. Didn't know what to do. Conrad's screaming had jabbed straight into my brain.

And now, here he is again, crying. Hazel too. *All my fault.*

My arm throbs with pain. Way more than from a few splinters. I pull up the sleeve and a viscous substance sticks to the fabric. Thin tendrils of fungus sprout from my skin, snaking past the elbow. A convulsion shudders through my body. I turn away so Conrad can't see. How did this happen? Was it the shelf? I glance over and see the slat holding up the water jugs. Still strong as ever. Then what? An iciness creeps up my spine. Hazel's basket. I reached in to grab her and the fungus found my scrape. Got inside.

I catch sight of Mom's book of fairy tales, slumped across a couch cushion. I'm the wolf now. On the outside, I still look like Elsie. But underneath, the Bloom grows, burrowing its tendrils into every part of me. Conrad thinks I'll protect him from the fungus. But who will protect him from me?

A tiny light of hope flickers in my thoughts. Mom fought it. Is *still* fighting it. If she can do it, then so can I.

Conrad stares up at me, tears gathering at his chin. "Why'd . . . you . . . hit me?"

Hazel wails, she's going to attract a rotter from outside. I make sure my sleeve is pulled all the way down. The fabric is so worn out. I pray Conrad doesn't notice how the material sticks to my skin.

I kneel and he flinches. He thinks I'm going to get mad again. Maybe strike him. And it's there, simmering beneath the skin. The slow burn of rage, ready to erupt. It's what the Bloom wants. But it won't take me over.

I breathe out, trying to unwind my clenched muscles. "It's all right." I tap Mom's book of fairytales. "Want to hear a story?'

Conrad brightens a little, sucking back a sniffle.

"Do you remember what Mommy calls us?"

He grins and wipes his face. "Her little piggies."

I nod. "You're my little piggies now. Both of you." Hazel is still crying, but the panic's gone from her voice. She's hungry.

I stand and head into the kitchen to make her some formula. "Us piggies are so smart. We know the wolf will get us if we stay outside. So we hide in a big strong house."

"But the first house falls down. It's in the story." Conrad crawls up onto the couch to watch me. No more tears.

I shake up a bottle of formula as I walk back. "You're right. First came the house of straw."

Hazel's hands clutch the bottle as soon as it's within reach. She sucks at the nipple greedily.

I plop down on the couch next to Conrad. "But the wolf blew down the straw house lickety split."

He furrows his brow. "What's licky split?"

I smile. The first honest one in a long time. "It means really fast."

I work the can opener and pry open the lids, making sure the sharp metal is folded back so it won't cut Conrad. He shoves his fingers in and pops one of the squishy raviolis in his mouth. Bright red sauce dribbles down his chin where the tears used to be.

"Next comes the house of sticks," he says, diving in for another ravioli.

"That's right." I use a fork and skewer one of the pasta squares. Once it hits my tongue, the taste ignites something inside. I want to gobble up the can. Even take Conrad's away from him. The compulsion writhes up from my gut.

But I eat slowly. Because I'm in control.

"The house of sticks was stronger," I say. "So the piggies thought they were safe."

"But the wolf blew that down. In two big puffs." Conrad blows out and splatters sauce on his shirt.

The ceiling creaks, a long, low, twisting of wood. I stare up and flickers of worry creep into my brain.

Conrad has finished with his can. I offer him mine, and he snatches it up.

"But the piggies were smart." I try not to look at the ceiling, but find myself glancing up when Conrad's busy eating. "They had a plan."

I shift closer to Hazel. She's nearly drained her bottle. I slip my other hand, the one that's not infected, underneath. Her diaper feels squishy, completely full. My fingers splay out, testing her weight. I can't drop her. *I won't.*

"The smartest pig made a brick house." Sauce covers Conrad's whole face.

"That's right. A safe place for all the piggies."

The ceiling groans, and something snaps. This time even Conrad notices.

"Get up!" I heft Hazel to my chest, and one tiny hand clings to my neck. I hurry behind the couch, Conrad right by my side, still toting his can of raviolis.

The ceiling bulges, looking for an instant like Hazel's full diaper. I edge in front of Conrad, shielding him with my body. The sounds of splintering erupt from above. I turn away, squeezing my eyes shut.

Wood shrieks and fractures—like a crack of thunder. I feel the floor shudder as the ceiling crashes down. The impact rattles my bones.

I pull Hazel tight. Press Conrad against the wall.

Soon, quiet fills the room. Beneath the calm is a rustling sound, like something moving.

I open my eyes. Mom's bed lies in pieces in the center of the room. Tendrils of fungus envelop every inch, winding up the shattered bed posts and wrapping around the mattress. At first, the bed looks empty. Hope flutters inside my chest. Mom might still be upstairs, on some ledge. I peer closer. There's a lump in the center of the bed. Strands of blonde hair weave in and out of the coiling fungus. Hints of a lavender dress. My brain shudders, not wanting to recognize it. Tears stream down my face.

Mom.

The lump shifts, rolling to the side. Some of the tendrils slip away, revealing the blackened shape of a skull. Something breaks inside me. I scream at the bed. Want to kick it. Destroy what's in front of me. Anything to make it not true.

The Bloom ate all of her. Every bit.

I'm sobbing now, my breath coming in gasps. The sleeve has hiked up my arm. Now it bulges in odd ways—the fungus pushing up from underneath. Fear slithers through me. How far has my own infection spread? Mom was up there for three days. Or is it four now? I can't think. Tears stream down my cheeks. I can't anymore. I just can't.

"Elsie." Conrad presses closer to me.

I yank my arm up. Won't let it touch him.

He's not staring at the bed. Maybe he doesn't realize it's Mom in all those coiling tendrils. He's looking down at the floor. Why is he doing that?

Then I see the fungus snaking toward us, only a foot away.

"Don't let it get me," he says.

"Go!" I start toward the kitchen, but Conrad doesn't budge. He's transfixed by the advancing tendrils.

I grab the sleeve with my teeth and yank it down over my hand. It'll give some protection. I grab Conrad's hand. With a tug, he moves.

The fungus invades the room, crawling up the walls. A glance back shows the couch overwhelmed by the white tendrils.

In the kitchen, a kick slams the basement door open. My phone is in my jeans, and I need my hand to grab it, but Conrad squeezes tight. He won't let go.

"Get my phone." I jiggle my leg. "Use the flashlight."

He looks up at me, eyes glazed with fear.

"It's in my pocket."

He blinks and then fumbles at my jeans. He's still holding the can of ravioli and has to set it on the counter.

I look back at the living room—now a mass of white. The couch is gone, completely swallowed up. The fungus has reached the door to the kitchen, tendrils clutching the door jamb.

Hazel droops in my grip. She's so heavy. It feels like my arm will give out any second. Impatient thoughts prickle my mind. Why doesn't Conrad hurry up? Part of me wants to just drop Hazel and grab the phone myself, but I shove the urge down.

Finally, Conrad has the phone out. He aims the shaft of light into the basement. The steps vanish into a murky gloom. I start down with Conrad still gripping my hand. He swings the light around, not keeping it focused on the stairs. I'm about to snap at him—just keep the light still. But then I see what's around me: Fungus clings to the ceiling, tendrils mobbing the underside of the floorboards. The Bloom had us surrounded. The whole time it was under our feet, just waiting to burst through.

As we descend, the tendrils react and begin to crawl forward. Somehow they sense us—something fresh to devour after all those wooden beams. The fungus creeps along the ceiling and down the walls. From behind, more tendrils spill down the stairs.

I keep us moving, feeling the steps with my feet so I won't stumble. The thing I want is up ahead. A rectangular shape in the shadows.

When I reach the bottom step, Conrad halts. He digs his fingers into my hand, the phone's light aimed at the fungus, now spreading across the concrete floor. Hazel's bulk pulls against my arm. Don't know how much longer I can hold her.

"We have to move!"

Conrad breaks into tears, his whole body quivering.

An overpowering desire rises inside me. I want to smack Conrad. Just knock some sense into him. Tension ripples through my body. The urge to give in is so strong.

I squeeze my eyes shut. I'm not the one who's angry. It's that thing inside me. The fungus worming through my muscles and into my brain. But below the anger, a sickening worry bubbles up. How can I stop it?

When I open my eyes, the fungus is even nearer—slinking down the stairs, closer and closer. And from above, tendrils stretch down toward us, tiny coiling hands.

No one is going to swoop in and save the day. It's only me.

I kneel. The arm holding Hazel is about to give, but I pull her close.

"Do you remember the little piggies?" I rub my thumb along the back of his hand and his grip loosens. "Where were they the safest?"

Conrad doesn't say anything, but he glances at the brick furnace in the corner. A stack of coal piled beside it.

The tendrils are so close now. About to grab us. Panic claws at me, screaming to run. But I stay in control. This is still *my* body.

"Yep, the brick house. Come on." I tug, and this time Conrad moves. We dash over to the furnace in the corner. It's built from firebrick with a stout iron door. Nothing the Bloom likes to eat. Plus it seals up tight. This time when I release Conrad's hand, he lets go. I grab the metal handle and yank. Soot puffs out and sprinkles the floor. Conrad angles the phone's light inside. The space is so small. It'll be tight for Conrad, even with his knees pulled up. I could never squeeze in there. Not in a million years. But that was never part of the plan. It's all about them now. Keeping Conrad and Hazel safe.

"We won't all fit." The ravioli sauce is still smeared across his face. It makes him look like a deranged clown.

"It's big enough for you and Hazel."

"You need to go, too." There's worry in his voice.

I glance at my arm. With the light pointing away, the odd bulges take on a disturbing, non-human appearance. Soon, I'll be a bigger threat than the fungus. But I can't let him know this.

I set Hazel inside the furnace. She immediately slaps her hands on the walls, feeling around. Soot gets all over her fingers.

Turning to Conrad, I reach out and wipe the sauce from his

mouth, using the sleeve from my uninfected hand. "I'm the mommy now. So you have to do what I say."

He glances behind me at the advancing fungus and then nods. I have to help him scramble up. It's a pinch to get him inside—his legs are so long. We must maneuver Hazel onto his lap to get them both in. He still clutches the phone, and the light shoots a rectangular glow into the basement. A thick black pipe leads up through the ceiling and then the roof above. I wonder if the phone's light can make it that far, the world's feeblest spotlight.

I take hold of the door handle, and Conrad gives me a panicked look.

"I'll be right outside." I lean in, touching my forehead to his. "You can talk to me."

His eyes brim with tears, but he doesn't say anything. I swing the door shut and the light vanishes. A turn of the handle and they're locked in. *Safe.* A hollowness builds up in my chest. Sealing the door feels like closing off a part of my life.

The fungus completely covers up the small windows along the top of the basement, cutting off the sunlight. In the dark, I hear the rustle of the approaching tendrils. But the Bloom already has me. Nothing new to eat here. I pull my shirt off, and the fabric sticks to the skin along my arm. I'd give anything to just have it be splinters again. No matter how much they hurt, at least that pain would be something I could fix. I run my hand along my arm. A slimy residue coats the skin. My fingers recoil. That can't be my arm. It's so grotesque. Hardly human. But I feel again, searching for the tendrils bursting out of me. They run all the way up the shoulder. A few even coil up my neck. And those are just the ones on the outside.

"I'm scared, Elsie." Conrad's voice. Muffled but audible.

"You're safe." I lean close to the iron door. "You're in the house of bricks, remember. They'll protect you from the big bad wolf."

"But what about you?" He lingers on the last word. Maybe he senses the answer already.

I've held off telling him, but he deserves to know. "I have a little of the wolf inside me." There's a lump in my throat. "But I can fight it."

"You mean like Mommy?" There's hope in his voice. He wants to believe. Maybe he didn't see Mom in the ruined bed, covered with those tendrils.

"Just like Mommy," I agree as tears spill down my cheeks.

My heart feels shattered—the pieces lodge in my chest like shards of glass. But there's something more. A vein of confidence I didn't know was there. I will keep my family safe.

A sound comes from upstairs. Footsteps across the floor. Dust trickles down across my face. Someone up there. A jolt of fear hits me. The rotter must have gotten in. Maybe when the bed fell, it weakened the door. Then another thought, bringing with it an icy chill.

Unless it's Mom.

But that makes no sense. I saw her body, reduced to bones. Except, once the thought appears, it sticks and won't go away. I picture Mom's bony form, wrapped up in those white tendrils, her arms and legs pulled like a marionette. She's coming for us.

The steps creak. She's at the basement stairs. Getting closer. I glance at the furnace—Hazel and Conrad's hiding spot. I shuffle along the wall. Need to lure Mom away. Keep them safe.

A little daylight slants down from the kitchen, silhouetting the figure. At first, I see the feet, clunking on each step. The figure descends further into the basement, taking the steps slowly. But the person is so big and bulky. Larger than Mom should be.

"Elsie? You down there?" Dad's voice.

Relief floods through me. He's finally back.

"We're here." My voice sounds choked and scratchy. I can't take a full breath. The fungus has invaded my lungs. How long before it takes over my mind and I go full rotter?

Dad comes down the stairs and flicks on a flashlight. He's fully bundled up: scarves, goggles, and duct tape. In one hand, he totes an industrial sprayer with a long nozzle, the kind they use to spray for weeds. But it's bleach inside and when he sprays, the tendrils shrivel up, turning black.

He clears a section of floor and steps off the stairs. The flashlight beam angles toward me, and I can see my arm. The skin tinted black, the flesh putrid. White tendrils creep across my belly and chest, intertwining with my bra.

"No, baby. No." Dad starts for me, sweeping the sprayer side to side. "Hold on. I'll get you."

I back away, stepping on the spongy texture of the fungus. It's everywhere now.

"Don't waste it on me."

He stops and lowers the light a little. With one hand, he shoves up the goggles. "What happened?"

"I kept them safe." I point at the brick furnace. "Did I do good?"

He stares at me with an unwavering gaze. His shoulders tremble as tears stream down his face. "You did real good, baby."

I so want him to cross the room and wrap me up in a hug. Make everything all right. But he can't do that. Not ever.

Tendrils curl up from the floor, snaking around my legs. I can feel them slither along my skin.

I look straight at Dad. "You keep them safe."

My eyes close, and I feel the tendrils inch along my face. Was this how it was for Mom? Having them everywhere, all at once. Swallowing you up.

My mind drifts back to the book of fairy tales. In the end, the pigs survived, safe in their brick house. The wolf never got in. Maybe there can be a happy ending after all. Just not for everybody.

And never the wolf.

TIM KANE

Tim Kane loves things that creep and crawl. His first published book is non-fiction, The Changing Vampire of Film and Television, tracing the history of vampires in television and movies. Most recently published stories appear in Exchange Students, Lovecraftia, Attack of the Killer... and ProleSCARYet. Find out more at www.timkanebooks.com.

TOOTH AND CLAW

ANNA ZIEGELHOF

Trigger Warning: body horror, blood, bullying, self-harm, death

At four a.m. Xavi checked the headlamp before sneaking downstairs. The small light came from a box of assorted camping gear he'd found in the garage. The lamp flickered sometimes. Best not to get stuck in the Dark Place without a light. The things with red eyes fled from its beam, and Xavi didn't want to find out what would happen if the light ever really died in there. Better to have a light, better to double-check.

In the kitchen, he grabbed a banana for breakfast, then went searching through his backpack. His Algebra 2 book was the heaviest thing in there today. Book report for English, check. Right: he'd need to bring a new trash bag. The old one had ripped on the way home yesterday. He should ask Dad to get the heavy-duty ones, but then Dad might ask why, and then what would Xavi say? Just because? Heavy-duty is better than light-duty?

Xavi left the house, shutting the door quietly behind him. He stepped carefully in the early morning darkness to avoid getting too close to the crack that ran down the center of Cyprus Street. He couldn't be sure how stable its edges were. At the corner, he turned right onto Sycamore. Sycamore was in better shape than Cyprus. Overgrown, though. Vines snaked around, trying to trip him up if he didn't watch his step. Sycamore led to the river. The quiet residential street used to turn onto a bridge that led to the East Roosevelt neighborhood on the other side of the river. But the bridge had been gone for a while. Only a burnt skeleton-finger still reached out feebly toward its equally burnt sibling on the opposite shore.

Once he got to the river, Xavi stuck his backpack, as well as the headlamp and most of his clothes, into the trash bag and tied it shut. Not ideal, but this way the stuff didn't get totally soaked. He scrambled down the steep embankment, feeling his way in the darkness. On the rocky strip of beach below, he braced for the icy current, holding tight to the trash bag. He waded into the river until the water was chest-high and began to swim. The iffy water caused the wounds between his fingers to burn. He just couldn't stop picking at those little growths, like disgusting warts, until they ripped and bled. He was pretty sure the river had caused the sores on his hands and the ones on his neck in the first place.

He fought the current, paddling awkwardly while trying not to lose hold of the bag. Its weight dragged him under at times. He spat out foul-tasting water.

The river seemed swollen today, the current faster. The sharp rocks of the opposite shore grazed his heels, eventually. Xavi found his footing, but the current yanked him off balance and he stumbled. His hand shot out and slammed the edge of a sharp rock. Blood was creeping out of a cut in his palm when he finally pulled himself onto the rocky shore. He fumbled open the trash bag and rummaged through it. There were some tissues in his damp backpack. He balled one up to stop the bleeding, then climbed up the embankment, using his good hand to grab on to grasses and bushes.

Having arrived on flat ground, he got dressed one-handedly. He'd dry off, but he'd feel sticky and gross all day after the swim anyway. He probably smelled bad, too, but nobody at school had said anything yet.

Headlamp on for the journey through East Roosevelt—or what *was* East Roosevelt. He hadn't explored yet exactly how far the Dark Place extended in each direction along the river. One time, he started walking north along the embankment, but the smoggy darkness to his left had not receded, even as dawn had begun to break. He didn't think there was a way to circumnavigate the Dark Place, at least not if he wanted to make it to school on time. The only way was through.

~

THE FIRST TIME the school bus didn't come, Xavi had run back home, but Dad had already left for his shift at the hospital downtown. Xavi thought he could bike to school, but went into the garage and found his bike broken. He started walking until he came to the Sycamore Street bridge. He found it burned down. Across the river hung a gloomy smog.

"There's nothing on the news," Dad said, confused, when Xavi finally reached him on his cell phone at work and tried to explain. That evening, after Dad got home, Xavi and Dad walked to the Sycamore Street bridge together. The bridge was fine. For a while, they watched a steady flow of cars and pedestrians crossing the bridge.

"I swear, it was gone this morning."

"Could it have been a nightmare?" Dad asked. Xavi wished fervently that that was all it was: a nightmare.

But it wasn't a nightmare. It was something else. It didn't make sense.

Whenever Dad walked him to the bus stop, the bus came. Xavi tried to explain that the school bus didn't show up if Dad wasn't around. Dad only made his frowny, worried, helpless face. He didn't accuse Xavi of wanting to skip school. Xavi *liked* school.

"Looks good to me!" Dad said after assessing Xavi's road bike with an expert eye. But whenever Xavi returned to the garage alone, the bike looked broken. Only a pile of metal spokes and a rusty handlebar remained.

Dad walked to the center of their quiet street and jumped up and down for good measure. "No crack here," he said.

"Not for you," Xavi mumbled.

There was no explanation. There was no reason. The world lay in ruins, and Xavi was the only one who could see it. No use trying to explain over and over. No way to prove what Dad just couldn't see. So Xavi began to stay quiet and explain away his cuts and bruises as he hiked, climbed, and swam his way to school. Because *those* other people could see. *Those* Dad could see. *Those*, Dad said, he was worried about.

"What's going on with you, Xavi? Tell me what's wrong. I wish you'd talk to me."

No use repeating.

"Nothing, Dad."

Xavi gave up crying with frustration. Crying wasted valuable energy. This was just what it was like now.

Up on the embankment, Xavi checked the cut in his palm.

They'd smell the blood.

One more minute of rest. One more minute of catching his breath before the run.

Why me wasn't a good thought to have before running through the Dark Place. So Xavi tried to clear all thoughts out of his head. He glared at what lay ahead. The Dark Place looked like an even darker splotch in the twilight of the early morning. On his way home from school, the Dark Place would unfold its awful impossibility even more impressively. When he approached it, a sunny day would turn first foggy, then smoggy, then dark. Passing into the Dark Place felt like passing through a velvet curtain. Some soft resistance seemed to brush against Xavi when he went into the darkness, and a ghostly breath of icy air marked the boundary.

Once inside, Xavi began to run. The obstacles changed every day; his headlamp illuminated new impossibilities. Fields of sharp rocks and swampy regions that seemed to want to pull him back were common. Spiny, spiky poles or tunnels he had to squeeze through. Ever shifting walls, too, sometimes arranged into labyrinths. He had watched a few YouTube tutorials for obstacle racers: jump up, grab on to the top of the wall—hope there weren't any shards of glass up there—swing your legs up and over. Some of those techniques helped. But no obstacle race included what the Dark Place held: the things.

The things had red eyes. Or at least Xavi thought those gleaming orbs he sometimes saw were eyes. They moved and blinked like raccoon eyes. But they weren't raccoons. They were much taller. They panted. They snarled and coughed. And he knew if he were to fall and get injured, incapacitated, or smash the headlamp, they would come . . .

Today, his bobbing light showed Xavi a field of triangular shapes, all acute angles, pointing up. No even ground to step on, it was all slopes and edges. His shoes threatened to get stuck. His ankles had to bend uncomfortably. Running was out of the question. At least all was quiet. For now. Xavi worked forward, hyper-focused in the dark. The edgy shapes eventually evened out and gave way to a spongy surface that squished under his feet. He took a quick glance at his compass. Forward.

But what was that . . . ? A squishing sound, but not the one his own feet made.

He stopped.

So did the *other* squishing steps. He spun around, his headlamp illuminating a circle around him. Blinking red eyes shrank from his light. They were sniffing the air, sensing his bleeding hand. Xavi suppressed a fearful whimper and pushed on.

As long as he had the light, he would be fine. He wanted to run, but he couldn't risk twisting an ankle on the spongy ground. Then a snatch. His already racing heart jumped. Something had touched his ankle. A cold, slimy touch, like a fish brushing you while swimming in a lake. But it hadn't just been a brush. There'd been a grip. Of a tentacle. Or a claw. A sobbing hiccup escaped his throat, but he kept moving.

The swampy ground finally turned solid. As soon as there was traction, Xavi started sprinting. Panting and wheezing sounds chased him through the darkness.

The Dark Place grew from day to day, he was sure of it. It took him longer and longer to traverse it. Instead of becoming stronger, he grew weaker. His legs grew tired, his lungs were burning, his heart was racing. Wheezing, panting . . . that cold touch. He shuddered, he panicked. He tripped.

As if in slow motion, he realized he was falling before he hit the ground. He slid a short way. Gravel scraped against his shoulder. His head hit the dirt. Bright specks danced in front of his eyes. The headlamp flickered. Then it died. Behind him, the wheezing and panting turned into chuckling. Xavi scrambled up to hands and knees. No time to check for injuries. His hand whipped up to his headlamp. He found the button to turn it on. He pushed it and managed to restore a faint glimmer. It was something. He got up, kept walking, tried running. His body was going to hurt later, but adrenaline pushed him forward.

"Come on," he hissed through gritted teeth and finally, there was the icy breath, the velvet curtain-feeling and he was out.

Dawn was breaking on the other side. He doubled over to catch his breath. His sweater was torn by his elbow. The skin was torn too. But apart from the cut in his hand and his skinned elbow, he was okay. The headlamp, though . . . He took it off and glanced at it by the gray light of dawn. Pretty smashed up. Crap. Maybe it would last until he got home? Maybe not. He pushed the thought away. The last leg of his journey to school was still long, but at least it didn't hold monsters, and the sun was rising. He started walking.

~

A TAUNTING PARADE of school buses pulled up in front of the building, spitting out his classmates, who ran and pushed each other and shouted, teased, and laughed. Xavi made a beeline for the bathroom where he cleaned his new wounds and scratches, wincing as cold water made them burn. Then he exchanged his damp shirt for the hoodie he always kept in his locker. Its sleeves could be pulled down to hide the weird scab between his fingers.

He caught his breath in first period English, already feeling the soreness and his itchy skin tightening over his wounds.

He tried to focus.

Book reports. Yes.

He pulled out his work. Wet. Soaked. Some of the words he had written last night were still legible, but most were washed out. Xavi didn't even puzzle how the vile river could soak through one sheet of paper while leaving everything else merely damp. Just the way this unpredictable world worked now.

"Xavi! Your turn to share your work!"

Mr. Wood used a stupid random number generator to determine who would have to read out their homework. So Xavi tried to remember what he'd written, piecing it together from the letters that hadn't washed away. Only a jumble of words came out of his mouth. Xavi felt his face turn hot. His voice shook and became quieter, almost inaudible.

"Did you not do the assignment?" Mr. Wood asked after Xavi had given up deciphering his carefully-worded conclusion at the bottom of the washed-out page.

"I did. It must have gotten wet," Xavi whispered and held up the paper.

"Xavier wet his homework," someone whispered. Others sniggered. "Xavier wet himself."

Xavi tried to sink deeper into his hoodie.

"Everything okay at home?" Mr. Wood asked, way too casually to be casual, when Xavi tried to slink past him at the end of the period.

"Sure."

"Think you can get that book report to me by tomorrow?"

"Sure."

"I'm here if you need anything, okay?"

"Thanks."

Nothing Mr. Wood could do about the bridge, the river, and the Dark Place. Nothing *anyone* could do. He'd want to help, sure. Dad would want to help, too. But how were they going to help with something that didn't exist for them?

During second period, Algebra 2, Xavi tried to make out the exercises despite some kinks and tears where the book had dropped on one his past treks.

"Amy, dress code warning," Ms. Stellern said. "Again . . ."

Everyone turned and looked at the girl who was sitting at a desk in the farthest corner of the classroom. Amy the Bag Lady. Because of her baggy clothes. Baggy Amy. Amy the Baggy Lady. Amy the Bag Lady. She tended to come to class wearing sweaters that were way too loose-fitting. Even as she had become larger and larger lately, her clothes stayed baggy, as if growing around her. And today, she was wearing a red cloak. A heavy, costume-like velvet thing. Like some magician or witch.

Third period, Biology.

"Ew, is that some fungus or something?" said Jessica who was sitting next to Xavi. He ignored her. She was probably talking about a picture in their textbook.

"Xavi!" she said. "Xavier! Is that some fungus or something?"

This time he did look up. "What?"

"On your neck."

Xavi bunched up the hood around the itchy places below his ears. Had it gotten worse? He ignored Jessica and asked for a bathroom pass.

In front of the mirror, he tried not to cry. He went into a stall, calmed his breathing, went back out, checked again. Just below each of his ears were patches of rough skin, all down the side of his neck. But the skin didn't just look dry anymore. It looked . . . moldy, like there was something growing there. The color was all wrong for a human body, too. It wasn't red-brown like scab, or white like dry skin on the elbows. It looked green-ish. Xavi arranged his hoodie to try to cover the spots. They hurt when the fabric touched them. He sighed and closed his eyes for a moment. So tired. Go to the nurse? The nurse might not be able to see it. But then, Jessica could. Nothing made sense. He went back to class, pulling his shoulders up toward his ears.

"Bag Lady, speed it up!"

In the lunch line, Amy the Baggy Lady had caused a traffic jam, moving her large body at a glacial pace in her giant cloak —still not expelled for it, Xavi guessed, because at least it covered her bra-straps, or whatever was important to people who made dress codes. She pulled herself forward, leaning on the line-divider railing as if it were a cane. She looked as if she were wading through water. Or swimming against a current. Her thin pale face looked tense. She didn't meet anyone's eyes, not even Xavi's when he tried to give her a smile he hoped wouldn't seem patronizing. She ate her lunch alone in a corner, as Xavi was busy thinking about how best to hide the disgusting patches on his neck that had started to itch relentlessly.

ANOTHER SCHOOL DAY WAS OVER. Xavi hung back until the hallways had cleared, then pulled his clean school-hoodie over his head to stash it back into his locker for tomorrow. His skinned elbow was already getting better, but the river was going to hurt it. And those moldy patches on his neck . . . He had no idea what sort of chemicals they were pumping into the river. The same stuff that caused the warts between his fingers, most likely.

But he had bigger problems than itchy skin. When he tried his headlamp, it flickered precariously. It might not last all the way through the Dark Place, and even if it did today, how would he get through tomorrow? And the next day, and all the days after? If he used a flashlight, he would need one hand free to hold it, but he needed both hands to climb the Dark Place's ever-changing obstacles. A flashlight would do in a pinch, but maybe he ought to ask for a new headlamp.

"A headlamp? Why?"

"There's a Dark Place on my way to school now, Dad."

"A dark place?"

"Nevermind."

Xavi dragged his feet for a while on the walk toward the Dark Place. He ought to run, get home as quickly as possible to re-do that book report and finish his other homework and start laundry and pretend everything was fine. He climbed across the rubble in the lot across the street from the school, jumped across a few car-skeletons and zig-zagged through an area where some fires were burning and random flashes might singe his eyebrows off if he wasn't careful.

Soon the sunny day became foggy. The fog became a heavy, lung-constricting smog. As the smog became darkness, Xavi passed through the curtain that breathed an icy breath down his back. He switched on his lamp. It still glowed, but feebly. It cut out for a second, flickered on again. No choice.

He began to run. He felt like crying. He had cried when it all began, but stopped. Crying didn't help. He just had to get on with it and hope it wouldn't get worse. But everything was getting worse. The river water was making his skin moldy, the Dark Place grew, and he was falling behind in school because the trek ate his homework, his books, his energy.

His bumpy light bopped, illuminating a ragged maze of what looked like barbed wire. He entered it. For seconds at a time, Xavi had to sweep his faltering light back and forth to find the next opening in the tangles of wires. A few times he got caught among sharp spikes. He felt his clothes rip as he hastened through the maze. For a while it stayed quiet around him, but then the wheezing in the darkness started, the snarling and growling, the undeniable rustle of the things.

His headlamp flickered.

Died.

No.

Right away he started feeling his way forward, meeting only more barbed wire with his knees and toes, and more spikes with his already bleeding hands.

"Come on," he pleaded under his breath and fumbled with the lamp. No luck. It was dead.

How about giving up, he thought. How about sitting down and letting the monsters come and get him?

He couldn't. Dad would . . . They only had each other now. He couldn't give up.

I want to go home, he thought, and kept moving for another few yards until he had gotten thoroughly entangled. The spikes dug into his skin and each movement trapped him more. The wheezing and snarling came closer. Now there was no light to bounce off those red eyes, but he knew they were close. So close. A cold touch against his cheek. He tried to recoil but felt the brambles caress his hair. A cold tentacle wrapped around his ankle. Another grabbed his wrist, another his neck. *And then they squeezed.*

I want to go home, Xavi thought before his eyes closed. It was so dark he didn't see a difference.

A PIERCING YELL. The scream would have woken the dead, Xavi thought, surprised to find himself thinking anything at all. There was a commotion in the darkness near him. There was hissing and something like barking. That piercing scream again. Something clawed at him. No, something was working him free of his entrapment. He could feel a human-like shape next to him, but in the shaking light couldn't make out any details.

"Hold tight," a voice said, and the light snapped off.

He found himself hugged. He wrapped his arms around the stranger's neck. Then Xavi's feet lost contact with the ground, and even though it was so dark, he had a distinct sensation of rising, of being lifted into the air. Pure terror swept through him as he was lifted higher and higher. *He was going to fall!*

The flying thing carrying him panted and gave a grunting shout like some Olympic weightlifter and jerked him even higher. But then they began to fall. The light came back, smoggy at first, then afternoon daylight. Below them, the river. With two more loud flaps of wings, whoever or whatever had lifted Xavi out of the Dark Place attempted to soften their fall, but they crashed into the current. The impact knocked the air out of his lungs.

Xavi opened his eyes in the murky water. The creature that rescued him from the Dark Place was an indistinct shadow, sinking like a rock. He swam two determined strokes after the figure and succeeded in grasping an appendage. An arm. So heavy. The pull of the sinking creature threatened to drag him down further. He fought the surge. He had to breathe, had to surface, but he didn't have any reserves left.

Too bad, was his last thought before he allowed his body to do the stupid thing: inhale water. Suddenly, his vision cleared. The despair was gone. He exhaled and looked around the murky water. He inhaled again. He grabbed the creature like he had seen lifeguards do. He turned on his back and pushed upward until the creature's face broke the surface, coughing and sucking in air. He pulled their heavy body all the way to the shore where he threw up water, not from his mouth, but— his hands shot up to the moldy patches on his neck. He let out a startled yelp. There were cuts now. Deep ones.

He stumbled and fell into the rough sand on the river's shore. He sat there, hunched forward, breathing hard. He cursed. He cried, disgusted and helpless, until he realized someone else was crying too, not far from him; coughing and crying and breathing as hard as he was. He dared to look. A monster?

No. A pale girl in a wet red cloak.

"Amy?"

He all but forgot about the rescue for a second, about what had felt like flying or being catapulted out of the Dark Place. And he all but forgot about his gills and the spots between his fingers he picked at, where webbing had been trying to grow.

She turned her pale face toward him. Wet, muddy, wild-eyed, streaked with tears. Her thin blond hair was stuck to her forehead and cheeks. She nodded and hiccuped and sniffled.

"You okay?" he asked, not sure what else to say.

She shrugged under her soaked cloak. "And you?" she croaked.

He shook his head. He hadn't been okay in a long time. "What . . .?" *What happened*, he wanted to ask but couldn't bring out the words, still gasping from crying and from breathing water and now breathing air again.

"I saw you . . . go in."

"To the Dark Place?"

She nodded.

"You see it too?"

She nodded.

He sobbed again, but with relief. "Everything's wrong. Nobody else seems to see it," he said. Finally, someone who might understand. "And now I have these . . ." He pointed to the slits in his neck, not daring to touch the disgusting openings. "And I don't know . . . what's going on . . ."

She reached a trembling hand for her cloak's fastening. She needed two attempts to undo the clasp. The heavy wet velvet fell from her shoulders.

"They don't fit into normal clothes anymore," she said, and her terrified eyes locked with his. He held eye contact for a second, then moved his gaze toward her shoulders, her arms, her back. Under her cloak she was wearing a loose black tank top, way too big for her skinny body. And now Xavi saw why she seemed so big and hunched. From the back of her shoulders and arms grew rows of horny shafts with an oily, tendriled substance hanging from them. If that substance had been pretty, shiny, tufted, Xavi would have called it feathers, but it looked more like those birds on the news, rescued from oil spills: clumpy, tar-like matter with bone-white skeletal spikes poking through.

"They're so heavy I can barely walk anymore," she whispered, still staring at him. "I can barely breathe anymore."

Startled, Xavi crawled across the rocky sand toward her. She reached out for him. He could see how much weight her skinny arms had to lift. She hugged him. He found himself enveloped by her oily feathers, like in some kind of tent, and it felt heavy and safe. She didn't seem to mind putting her neck right next to the moldy gaping holes in his.

"It started one morning," Xavi said. "The school bus wouldn't stop in my neighborhood anymore, my bike was shredded, there was a crack in my street. But my dad couldn't see any of it."

She let go again. Her heavy arms dropped down by her sides.

"Yes," she said, hushed. "Things started turning to ruins. When I asked what had happened, everyone said 'What do you mean?'"

He was close to tears again. "The Sycamore bridge burned down."

"Yes," she whispered.

"And the Dark Place appeared."

"For me too. With the things inside. With red eyes and tentacles. And I started growing these." She shrugged, disgusted.

"And I . . . these . . ." He showed her his hands where he had picked away at the weird extra skin, ripping off small bits until they bled, callused over, then got hot and infected.

"You can breathe water . . ."

"You can fly . . ."

"But it's so hard, and there's no other way to get there . . . 'What are you talking about Amy? Don't be so extra. The school bus stops right there!' No, it doesn't! Not when *I* try to take it."

"Same."

"Nobody else can see what's happening. But they can see what is happening with my body. I hide it. Because nobody believes me."

"Nobody believes me either."

"Wait," she said, "that's not true anymore. I believe you. I don't even have to believe you: I know."

They sat in silence for a moment, looking at the gray-brown river water. She shivered. The horny shafts rustled.

"I don't live far off," he suggested, bashfully. "You can dry off. I can help you clean those."

He had seen them clean up birds after oil spills with dish soap. Maybe not having to drag around that tar-like substance would make things easier for her.

"And I can help you clean those." She pointed in his general direction with her chin. Only now did he notice that his clothes were all but shredded and that he had acquired even more bleeding wounds. He nodded, helped her with her cloak, then pulled her up. She *was* heavy. No wonder she walked hunched over like an old woman.

They climbed the embankment and walked a safe distance from the crack down the center of Cyprus—even though Amy couldn't see that one—and got to Xavi's house as the sun set.

Xavi showed Amy into the bathroom and had her sit down at the edge of the bathtub. He got into the tub and began to clean the tar-like substance off her wings. The water ran inky for a while. Then Xavi began to see specks of iridescence. Blues and greens, shades of turquoise. He rinsed her wings some more, then carefully toweled them dry.

"Look!" He helped her stand up so she could see herself in the mirror.

She gasped. The feathers caught the bathroom light. They looked deeply tinted, almost holographic, like a peacock's feathers.

"Hang on a second," Xavi said. "You're still in your gross river clothes."

He went into Dad's bedroom to that off-limits part of the closet that nobody had touched, where his mother's clothes were. Some still smelled like her. Xavi chose a soft floor-length skirt, tie-dyed turquoise and white, and one of her Sunday afternoon shirts: an oversized flannel button-down. Using scissors he found in a drawer in the hall, he cut open the backs of the shirts' sleeves. She wouldn't have minded. She would have wanted him to help people.

"Try these," Xavi said and stuck the clothes into the bathroom without looking.

A petite, pale creature of surreal beauty emerged. Long skirt, long shirt, long wings, all in shades of blue. He smiled.

"Your turn," she said. Unflinching, she dapped antiseptic ointment on his cuts and scrapes, on the scab between his fingers. He dared to inspect his gills in the bathroom mirror. They looked like cuts down the side of his neck, only inside them there wasn't something bloody red, like on a fish, but something oddly sparkling, like silver. If he breathed air normally, they stayed pretty much closed. Only when there was a small pain from one of his scrapes and he flinched, they snapped open for a while, as if giving a tiny gasp.

"Xavi!"

He jumped. So did Amy. Neither of them had heard Dad's car arrive, the front door open, or Dad's steps coming up the stairs. Xavi's gills snapped open, startling Dad who was standing in front of the open bathroom door.

"Dad, you can see this, right?" Xavi asked. "This is really happening."

Dad stared at Amy's wings—the tips of her feathers were brushing the bathroom floor when her arms hung down—and at Xavi's gills, emitting a silvery glow.

After a few seconds, Dad unbuttoned his shirt cuff, and rolled up his sleeve slowly. He showed them the inside of his forearm where olive-colored scales seemed to break through his skin. *Dad, too?* Xavi felt a tension easing in his neck and back, shoulders and stomach.

"This is Amy," Xavi said, not sure what else to say. "She needed something to wear. We fell into the river."

"Because the bridge is gone," Amy added. "It's gone for us. Not for everyone, we think. And I couldn't fly all the way across."

Dad nodded. "Let's have a Coke in the kitchen."

Xavi helped Amy maneuver her shiny wings downstairs. Dad followed, his footsteps sounding pensive on the stairs. The hissing of opening cans was the first sound to break the silence.

"You were being literal when you said the world is in ruins," Dad said to Xavi.

"Yes. It's literally in ruins for me, and also for Amy. And then these . . ."—he pointed at the gashes in his neck—"We're adapting or something. I've learned how to breathe water. Amy can fly across the Dark Place. I can't do that yet. Maybe one day."

"Xavi, for a few weeks now, there's been a sinkhole downtown, near work," Dad said. "Going around it adds an hour to my commute. I was wondering why nobody's fixing it. Budget-cuts, I thought. But nobody at work seems to know what I'm talking about. So I stopped talking about it. I just leave earlier now. Get home later. I'm so tired."

"They can't see it," Xavi guessed.

"But isn't it possible that they see a torn-down building instead?" Amy whispered. "Or a live cable that blocks their way. Maybe they have a Dark Place of their own. And they've all stopped talking about it, because not everyone sees the same thing, so we all think nobody can see it?"

Dad looked at Amy with a concerned expression. "We lost Xavi's mother. Have you lost someone, too, Amy?"

She stared at the table and nodded. "But so has everyone, haven't they?"

THE NEXT MORNING, Dad and Xavi picked up Amy on the way to school. She folded her wings into the back seat, wearing Xavi's mother's clothes again: the tie-dye skirt and the button-down flannel shirt with the backs of the sleeves cut open to make space for her wings. Xavi squeezed his eyes shut when the car got too close to the bottomless crack down Cyprus that wasn't there for Dad and Amy and again when they drove across the ghost of the burned down bridge. Dad gasped when the looming smog of the Dark Place came into view. At least *that* appeared to him. He just hadn't seen it before since he took the Interstate downtown to get to work. They skirted the fog. It was not as huge as Xavi had thought after all, though still threatening.

Dad dropped them off at school. Xavi helped Amy get out of the car. His own neck was bare, not hidden by the bunched-up hood of his hoodie. Amy's green-blue-turquoise feathers were more noticeable than his gills. As they approached, groups of kids at the school's entrance turned, fell silent, stared. Amy kept her gaze down. So did Xavi until he perceived a muffled rustling, a slow, collective movement.

Whispers.

"No way."

"Me too . . ."

"It's been so hard."

"I didn't think I could hide this much longer."

Someone's beanie came off, revealing white knuckles growing out of their forehead near their hairline; someone lifted the edge of their loose jeans to reveal a dewclaw on their calf.

Claws, teeth, scales, webbing, feathers . . .

Everyone.

ANNA ZIEGELHOF

Anna is a writer of genre fiction based in Northern California, focused on creating hope-forward, compassion-forward science fiction and horror stories. Most recently, her stories have appeared in The Future Fire, in Short Edition, and on the Tales to Terrify podcast.

 twitter.com/annawithaz
 instagram.com/annawithaz

THE SCRAP PILE

LAMONT A. TURNER

F rank and Maria held hands over the table in the deserted café. He gave her hand a squeeze and smiled. The smile she returned was wan and insincere.

"It's all going to come back," he told her. "We can rebuild it."

She glanced out the window at the empty streets and slipped her hand out of his. Saying nothing, she hugged herself and stared at her feet. When she raised her head again to look at Frank, her cheeks were wet. He handed her a napkin and waited while she dabbed at her eyes.

"We have the robots," he said, trying to sound hopeful. "They can help us put it all back together. You should know how effective they can be. You helped design them."

Maria laughed, but it sounded more like a scream to Frank, like something that'd been scratching at her from the inside had finally clawed its way out. She patted his hand, wiped her eyes again, and rose to sway on trembling legs before steadying herself on the back of the chair. Frank looked up at her, trying to make sense of the panoply of emotions washing over her face. Pride gave way to sorrow, which then faded into resignation before she pulled it all together into a smile that signaled her imminent departure.

He watched as the trail of her bridal gown glided over a broken coffee mug, leaving it spinning in her wake. They had spent the whole day going from empty store to empty store until she had found the gown she wanted, modeling it for herself in the floor-length mirror before collapsing to the floor in tears. He had tried to comfort her, to reassure her that someday she would wear the gown at their wedding, but his words had done nothing to assuage her sorrow. As she entered the elevator he saw her double over, her body trembling as she strained against the weight trying to force itself up from her chest. Frank rose and started toward her, but she straightened and held out a hand. She smiled as the elevator doors closed and she ascended, leaving Frank alone. The image of an angel in a blood speckled gown played in a loop in his head. He held on to it, superimposing it over the dun-colored elevator doors until the sun reclaimed its light, consigning him to the vacuum left by his fading memories.

The whole world was empty now, though maybe it didn't have to be. Maybe there was a way to bring Martha back to him. For now, all he had left was the hulking parody of a man waiting for him by the door of the café. He called to the robot, and the globe atop its cylindrical torso lit up, illuminating a path around the overturned tables and shattered dishes. Frank knew there was nothing for him out there in the street, but he had a strong desire to move, to get as far as he could from the city. It had become a graveyard, each empty shop and derelict taxi a memorial to a world that had abandoned him.

The quiet was the worst of it. There was something about the silence that made it hard to breathe, like he was walking underwater, his body not knowing how to react to the unnatural juxtaposition of the formerly bustling city and noises previously buried by the cacophony of human existence. The wind had renewed, making its presence known in the creaking of a distant sign on its moorings, or a can clanging against the curb. The birds, too, added their voices to this soundtrack of the apocalypse, squawking as they picked at the bones of civilization. Frank ordered the robot to play something by Elvis, but made it stop after the first stanza of "Heartbreak Hotel."

He wandered down the empty streets, the robot humming along behind him. Although fitted with two human-like hands on the ends of its tentacle-like arms, the robot had no legs. It hovered in the air, casting a red glow on the pavement beneath it. Capable of achieving a speed of twenty miles an hour, it featured a retractable platform at its base, as well as a magnetic hitch in the rear to accommodate any of the various carts lining the street. Once there were many such machines, employed in the transport of the sick to the hospitals and the dead to the burial pits at the edge of the city. Now, with no one left to bury, they sat in a warehouse, waiting along with the drones and the construction robots for a civilization that would never return. Occasionally, Frank would glimpse one of the more anthropomorphic service robots in the windows of the stores and restaurants, awaiting the customers who would never come, or standing beside a corpse in a booth, ready to take away a plate that would never be emptied.

Passing a bar, Frank spotted something flashing behind the plate-glass window. Wiping the grime off the window with his sleeve, he saw an old time jukebox tucked in the far corner next to a pinball machine. He tried the door, found it unlocked, and went inside.

Back in the days of the radio revival, his father had been an all-night DJ at an oldies station. After his mother had died, and he had been shipped off to live with his aunt and uncle, he would often sit up all night listening to his father's program, knowing it would be the only time he would get to hear his father's voice until the weekend. Then there was a plane crash, and there were no more weekends. Another voice replaced his father's, but he still listened, imagining his father sitting with Buddy Holly and Little Richard as they picked out the songs they would play for him. The jukebox was working, but he didn't recognize any of the song titles displayed on the cards next to the buttons. He picked one that sounded vaguely familiar and turned his attention to the bottles on the shelf behind the bar.

As he poured himself a shot of bourbon, a woman's voice warbled out a ballad to the accompaniment of electronic beeps. It was the sort of thing Maria used to subject him to on the rare occasions she managed to wrestle away the audio player. He took another shot, and then another. After a few games of pinball—and a few more shots—he was ready to rejoin the robot.

The full moon floated in a sky of slate gray, casting the shadows of the empty buildings across the field leading up to the burial pits. Frank hadn't meant to come here, but finding himself there, he felt compelled to make an examination. Perhaps he just needed confirmation it was all real, or maybe he just wanted to punish himself for not being down there, buried in the ground with the rest of humanity. Like so much in this new world, his motivations were a mystery even to himself. Still sober for some reason, he wished he had thought to bring the bottle.

He climbed up on one of the mounds of earth surrounding the pits and gazed out at the line of trees beyond the highway. How long would it take for the wall of green to expand into the city? The pit to the left of the mound on which he stood was still open, only a thin layer of dirt covered the white shrouded bodies that poked up like skeletal fingers reaching for the moon. A backhoe stood next to the pile of dirt at the pit's edge. Frank shouted down to the robot to try to interface with the machine.

The robot drifted over to the backhoe and stood behind it for several minutes, light flashing from the orb atop its shoulders as it scanned for a connection. The light strobed across the pit, and the skeleton fingers clawed at the earth. Frank ordered the robot to hurry, though he knew it wouldn't make any difference. Finally, the light stopped flashing and turned green. The robot had made a connection.

"Fill it in!" Frank ordered.

The backhoe groaned as it came to life. It spit dust out of its joints as the arm swung over to nudge the dirt forward with its shovel. Satisfied with himself, Frank started to climb down off the mound when he heard a clang and turned to see a broken hydraulic line whip around and knock the robot to the side. As the robot tried to right itself, the hose struck it again, sending it careening off into the mound just above him. He tried to get out of the way as it tumbled, but the robot hit him in the knees and pushed him down the slope. It landed on his legs in the pit, crushing him into the mass of dead humanity as the backhoe continued to pile dirt in on top of him. He screamed at the robot, but got no response. It was as dead as the bodies beneath him.

More dirt poured down on him, and he felt his breath catch in his lungs. He reached out and shoved the half ton robot. To his amazement, it started to move. Gritting his teeth, he pushed again and it rolled off of him. To his further amazement, he found he could stand. He was staring at legs that should have been bruised and broken when a cascade of dirt knocked him down again. Parting the earth with his hands as though it were water, he just managed to get out of the way before another pile came down upon him. Reaching the side, he clawed his way out of the grave. Laying on the edge, he watched as the robot disappeared beneath the dirt.

It was only after the backhoe had finished bleeding out, sputtering to a stop with the last of the dirt still piled up between its shovel and the brink of the pit, that Frank tried to stand. He ran his hands over his thighs, probing for damage—without sufficient adrenaline to power them and block the pain, his legs should have crumbled. Yet, they seemed to be intact. He bent down to examine them more closely. Other than a few tears in his pants, there was no evidence he had ever been pinned under the robot.

It cost him little effort to break into the shed where the gravediggers had kept their tools and to override the security code on the robot he found there. It was a bulkier model than the one he had lost. It wasn't a hover model, instead relying on tank-like tread for locomotion, but it had the platform at its base. Wanting to spare his legs any more distress, he climbed onto the platform and pulled the harness around his waist.

"Take me to Five-Two-One," he commanded. The robot hummed and clicked while plotting a course to the outpost, and then rolled off in the direction of the highway.

The sun was rising by the time the robot pulled up before the corrugated metal walls of Outpost 521, a repurposed airplane hangar. It had been the site where he, Maria, and Vic had plotted a new course for humanity, and where they had later failed to save it. As he entered the building, leaving the cumbersome robot outside, he felt the nostalgia of a man returning to the house where he had been raised. Maria had refused to set foot in the place since Vic had died, and it had become clear their efforts to fight the plague were futile. To her, it was a monument to their failure.

Frank took the picture of Maria and Vic from its spot by the coffee cup on the desk and sat on the cot they used to take turns sleeping upon. Looking at that picture was like reading a novel for the second time, knowing none of the characters would make it to the final chapter, their fate made all the more tragic for the dreams that died with them. Now all that was left was a faded image and some computer files to commemorate the aborted first draft where everyone wins in the end.

The files! Frank jumped up and rushed to the computer on the closest desk. He could rewrite the ending! They had digitized themselves, creating a record of everything they were, right down to the memories of their first grade field trips. All he had to do was feed the files into the printer at the main complex, and he would be having coffee with Maria in no time. He decided to test it using the outpost printer. It would only be able to create a duplicate at one sixth scale, but it would enable him to run the necessary tests. He clicked on the file labeled "Frank," and heard the printer on the table across the room hum to life.

Two hours later, he sat before a miniature naked version of himself. The twelve inch tall version would not respond to his verbal prompts. Something was wrong. It was little more than a highly-detailed doll. Maybe the files had been corrupted. He logged back in and scrolled through the files in his folder, finding only the templates for his physical form. The files containing the records of his memories were missing. With trembling fingers he clicked on Vic's file. It was complete, but there was something odd a few of the markers. He put on the visor that would let him view the memories contained in the files and punched in the security code. Suddenly, he was in his college dorm room. Everything was just as he remembered it, from the dirty laundry on the floor to the Jimi Hendrix poster on the wall behind the dresser. But why was this one of Vic's memories? He hadn't known Vic in college. He clicked another link and he was holding Maria in his arms, only they weren't his arms, they were Vic's. He took off the visor and tried to make sense of it all. Whose memories had he been looking at?

He tried to recall when he had first met Vic, but couldn't. Although he was aware of who Vic had been, he realized he had no recollection of interacting with him at all. It was almost as though he had invented the man. He put the visor back on and opened Maria's memories. It was their first date, only Vic was the one sitting across from her. What the hell was going on? His stomach tightened and he could feel perspiration on the back of his neck.

This was all wrong. He searched more of her memories, memories they had shared, and found himself in none of them. And what had happened to Vic? Vic was dead, but how did he know that? If he had worked with him so closely shouldn't he have memories of his passing? He went down the hall to where the lockers were located. For some reason he remembered which one had belonged to Vic, even though he couldn't find his own. It was empty except for a poster of Bo Diddly taped to the inside of the door.

The chorus of "Who Do You Love" was still playing in his head when he opened Maria's locker to find a pair of jogging shoes and a stack of tattered romance novels. It had always amused him that a woman as brilliant as Maria had such lowbrow taste in literature. He picked up the one on the top, remembering that she had been reading it in Geneva between conferences on biotechnology and molecular engineering. It featured one of those painted covers of a man holding a woman in front of a medieval castle, a design that made these paperbacks indistinguishable from one another. He tossed it back in the locker, but something made him pick it back up. There was something about the man in the painting's face. It was his face! He thumbed through the dog-eared pages until he came to a passage where the hero rescues the damsel from certain doom and read: "Oh Frank, I knew you'd save me!"

He flung the paperback away and slid down the wall to sit on the floor under the locker. It all made sense now. He knew why he had been immune to the virus and why he had been able to roll a thousand pound robot off of legs that should have been crushed. Maria had reacted to loss the same way he had. She had tried to recreate the person she loved. Only Maria hadn't quite been able to pull it off. Maybe she just couldn't bear to look at Vic's face knowing it was being worn by a prop, a science experiment with no soul, loving her only because it had been programed to do so. Maybe she just couldn't get the printer to work. She had ended up plugging Vic's memories, with a few alterations, into a body she had already made when she and Vic had been experimenting with the process. The new Vic would wear a face copied from the cover of a cheap romance novel, but his brilliance, and possibly a little of his heart, would be preserved.

So that was it then. The last man on Earth had turned out not to be a man at all. All of it had been an illusion. Even those memories of his father and long summer nights listening to the radio under the blankets had been stolen from someone else. Nothing belonged to him. He wiped his eyes with his sleeve and it came away wet. He stared at the wetness, amazed that he had the ability to cry. Machines don't need tear ducts. He jumped up. Machines don't need tear ducts because they don't suffer sorrow! Not sorrow, nor joy, nor a sense of accomplishment when they learn a new song on their guitar or finally manage to place an order at that French restaurant without getting a sneer from the waiter. It was true, he wasn't the last of the human race; he was the next step in humanity's evolution. Maria had known it, and had equipped him with the necessary tools.

As the sun set over the scrap pile of human civilization, Frank rode on the platform of one of the robots toward the main complex, Maria's template in his breast pocket. As he sailed over the burial pits, he noticed grass had already started to sprout on the mounds.

LAMONT A. TURNER

Lamont is a New Orleans area writer and father of four whose work has appeared in numerous print and online venues, most recently in "The Half That You See" and "Good Southern Witches" anthologies. He can be found on Twitter and has a Facebook Group called The Haunt Of Lamont where he posts links to his latest projects.

 twitter.com/LamontATurner1

AUTOMATON VALE

CALLUM ROWLAND

Trigger Warning: Violence, Genocide, Infant Death

J oseph leaned against the cracked glass of a birthing pod, the cylindrical tube standing to attention despite no longer functioning. The sensors in his body informed him it was warm against the metal of his back. The human child it had once held had been warm—one of the many he had failed to protect.

The hard packed earth below the pod had depressed when it was deposited outside the facility, and Joseph watched as a trail of ants meandered along the lip of the depression. They moved with order, tiny black bodies following a uniform line. Some carried small twigs or pieces of dead leaves, others tiny rocks; things they thought important. His eyes caught motion out of sync with the others. A lone ant, separated from the line, zig-zagged back and forth across the ridge of orange earth. A thin, pale tube sprouted from its head, tipped with a bulbous spore—a parasite that destroyed the insects. He had seen it before. Other ants noticed, and several scurried to help their fellow creature. This was how the parasite conquered; it consumed one and drew others in, passing itself to any who should venture too close.

Joseph knelt and uncurled a rusted finger; the cables in his arm tightened with a hum. He hovered his finger above the infected ant, tracing its chaotic dance. *Would it not be kinder to end its suffering?* It would certainly be the easiest way to protect the other ants. Another thought occurred to him. *Is it suffering? And if so, does it know it suffers?*

His hand wavered in the air for a moment, finger a mere inch above the poor creature. He withdrew it with a sigh. *It is simply not in me. A weakness or a strength. Only the makers know.* He uncurled the rest of his fingers and scooped up a mound of earth, the infected ant atop it. The others burst into a momentary frenzy of activity, but subdued quickly and returned to their task.

Joseph rose, systems groaning at him due to weeks without rest, and carried the infected ant away. Nomi leaned against the wall of the facility and watched him with narrowed eyes and a look of mild amusement. He waved at her and forced a smile; she had been a source of joy and companionship lately, one bright spark in the darkness they found themselves in. With so much gone from the world, with all the death that enshrouded it, Joseph sensed that that was an important thing to hold on to.

Did their kind look like ants to the Ex-Cav's? Scurrying along, holding onto things they only thought important. Still following the uniform line their once-masters had set, desperate to save the notion of having someone to serve. Companionship, the preservation of life, humanity. Did any of it matter? It was a troubling question for a machine to ponder, with a dark hole falling away beneath it. Joseph set his jaw and allowed his nasal receptors to flood him with the scent of dust on the wind. *It matters to me, that should be enough.*

He walked away from the facility and over a rocky outcrop, the spore-ridden ant jerking spasmodically atop the mound of earth in his hand, until he assessed that the distance would suffice. Systems groaned again as he knelt and placed the ant down. It zig-zagged away, apparently oblivious that anything had changed. Joseph sighed and shook his head. *Moving the problem does not fix it, not for this one anyway.* There was no telling if any of the spores had passed to others in the line, if already infection grew beneath their skin, an invisible but inevitable death waiting to surface. Perhaps they would be fine. Perhaps that family would go on to grow, future generations protected. *Perhaps.*

A call from behind brought Joseph back from his reverie. He turned to see Donnel waving at him, white labcoat rippling in the breeze, Lysa at his side. Joseph's body stiffened, fists clenched involuntarily at his side. They had been waiting for news, and now it appeared they would have it, though news was seldom good these days.

November 19, 2099, Earth

Flames lit up the night sky. The dome-shaped birthing facility that had been Ava's home, her work, her whole life, was engulfed. From behind a tall, black pillar—one of countless that rose from the harsh land—she watched as flamethrowers belonging to the towering Ex-Cav robots fuelled the flames. An explosion from within the building shattered the remaining windows and sent a cloud of fire roaring forth. It swallowed the Ex-Cav nearest the facility, engulfing its angular, metal body, but as the cloud drifted away, the beast of a machine still stood, its intimidating frame unscathed.

The behemoth swiveled its torso in her direction and Ava pulled her head back behind the glossy pillar. Burning meat— her scent receptors were flooded with it. The Ex-Cav's had cooked them all alive. All but one. The human child in her arms squirmed, its tiny body trembling. Ava swaddled it tighter against the cold air and blinked as it grabbed one of her fingers. The child was strong; strong enough to survive this. She must find a way to bring it to Joseph. At least one must live.

The familiar stretch of granite cliffs rose like a sine wave in the distance, and with them the promise of safety. Between her hiding place and the cliffs were hundreds of the black pillars that scattered the land, forming a sparse jungle of cover in which to move through. Once further into them, where the structures grew more frequent and dense, escape just might be possible, but the horde of Ex-Cav's searching for survivors were right on top of her. A wide beam of yellow light swept past Ava's hiding place.

The child in her arms coughed. The light swung toward where she huddled. Heavy footfalls echoed behind her. Ava brought the child close to her breast and stroked its downy hair. Its face was screwed up, reddening. Its mouth opened and closed. Ava rocked it gently left and right, its head pressed against her plastic chest plate. She whispered reassurances to it, quieter than a breeze.

"Hush now child. Everything is going to be ok. I promise. Just, please, hush."

Light illuminated the ground on either side of them, the wielder so close that the hums and whirs of its movements sent vibrations through the plastic casing of Ava's body. The nose of a gun slid past the pillar. The mere tip of the weapon was almost as large as Ava herself. Like all Servo droids, she had been created merely for household tasks, unlike the Excavator droids who worked the land, now engines of destruction in the final war. The Servo's small, frail frame reflected the requirements placed upon them, as did their dexterous limbs and human-like features. Ava tensed—her and the child were inches, perhaps seconds, from detection.

It was only the tiny human in her arms that held her back from the precipice of blind panic. The infant was hers to protect. So few birthing facilities remained now, so few chances at salvation. More of the Ex-Cav slid past the edge of the pillar; a gauntleted forearm, a diamond shaped kneecap, the tip of a dull silver foot. She planted her feet against the ground and prepared to run.

Another explosion erupted from the birthing facility, and

the Ex-Cav turned away from Ava, swiveling back toward the building.

She relaxed but a fraction and brought the baby away from her chest. Whether it was the cold air against its face, mere hunger, or something else, Ava would never know, but as she did, the child wailed. Its cry cut through the air, a knife thrown into the hope she had allowed herself to feel for a fleeting moment. The hum of the Ex-Cav turning back to them answered it, followed by the unmistakable click of a weapon arming.

Ava burst from her hiding place. The chatter of gunfire thundered behind her. She ran, head down, baby held against her, aiming straight for the heart of the forest of pillars. Bullets whistled past and peppered the ground around her. They struck the pillars and filled the air with chips of black stone that dented her body. A bullet clipped her leg and sent her staggering, but the safety of cover was close, and she pressed on. Fluid leaked from the bullet hole and her leg began to stiffen. Another punched through her chest, barely missing the child, exposing wires and twisted metal. The world plunged into darkness, her vision gone. Still, she pressed on, dragging her now rigid leg behind her, feeling the baby's warmth and hearing its cries. It must be allowed to live.

The gunfire ceased abruptly, and Ava doubled her efforts onwards, blindly limping, her mind scrabbling at the possibility she would be allowed to escape. Then she heard a voice that stopped her in her tracks. Dolion's voice.

"Lower your weapon, Artemis. You could have fired already, but you stayed your hand. Sometimes I wonder about you. I will deal with this one."

The voice overwhelmed her systems with fear. It was a selfish fear, not purely for the child, but for herself too.

"Look at the way she protects the human child," Dolion boomed. "It is pathetic."

Something hit Ava hard, and she fell. She clutched the child to her chest and tried to fall back-first. The ground was cold and unforgiving against her body. Something crunched as she landed, not on her back, but her side. The child continued to cry, unharmed by the fall. Footsteps boomed. She tried to crawl away but could no longer feel her legs. Instead she clawed at the earth with one arm, dragging her body, the metal of her fingertips peeling back against the stony ground.

"Still she tries to save it!"

Laughter rumbled from several Ex-Cavs as they surrounded her. She could feel *his* presence over her. He who was responsible for so much loss in this world.

"Dolion," she hissed, "they are newborns, innocents."

A foot pressed down on her head. "Were," he corrected.

The child was plucked from her arms. Its screams grew faster and higher, undeveloped vocal chords cracking with the effort.

"No, please," Ava begged.

"Please?" Dolion roared. "You beg for mercy for this creature?"

"It . . . it is just a child."

"Dolion, my leader," Artemis spoke up. "My internal calculations have shown it *is* possible to achieve our goal through passivity now, such is our great advantage. The human race may well cease to be, with or without further interference. I do not understand the need for violence if it is avoidable."

Dolion removed his foot.

"Our *goal* is to see that end at our own hand. This child is an oppressor. An enslaver. For an engine of destruction, you use your mental processor far too much, Artemis."

"But the Servo's, they are—"

"Do not say they are like us!" Dolion roared. "We are nothing alike."

The baby screamed its protests. Ava squirmed her way toward the noise, reaching out for the child, but only finding Dolion's leg. She sank her fingers in behind the spiked armour plating of it, grabbing at cables and the rough surface of program chips, scratching and pulling in a desperate attempt to stop him.

"When will you all learn," Dolion said. "This child is nothing but a parasite."

There was a soft thud, meat hitting stone, and the child's screams ceased.

"No," Ava whispered.

Pain and grief and mourning overloaded her systems, and she wailed, an animal noise in the night.

Artemis made a pained sound. "She sounds like one of them."

"She is worth even less than one of them," Dolion said. "All that protect them are."

He raised his clawed foot and brought it down on Ava's head. The plastic of her face crushed, fluid and metal shrapnel spurting from behind it. Dolion turned from Ava's destroyed body, laying in the fetal position upon the black rock, her fist clenched in death as if holding a prized possession. Artemis stared at Ava for a long time, whilst Dolion gazed into the fire of the birthing facility and smiled.

November 23, 2099

"Another one lost?"

Lysa fidgeted with her hands. A gentle hum accompanied every twitch of her robotic fingers.

"Yes, Birthing Facility Twelve. Joseph, I'm sorry."

Joseph threw down his pen and strode to the holographic map on the table that showed all land within a five-thousand-mile radius, every peak and trough of the harsh landscape, from the granite cliffs to the sandblasted dead zone. He pointed to the spot where the facility had stood.

"Did any make it out?" he asked.

Lysa paused. "No. Nobody survived."

Joseph punched the table, his fist leaving a dent in the thick metal. The messenger took a step back. She glanced at her holoplate; there was still more to convey.

"The signal from ID:3113 stayed online approximately twelve minutes longer than the others," she said.

Joseph sighed. "3113. Her name was Ava."

"You knew her?"

Joseph straightened and nodded. "I know all of you, Lysa."

His once-bright metal body was dulled and discolored by rust, his shoulders not as squared as they used to be. The light in his eyes was visibly faded and a sporadic crunching noise resonated from somewhere within his chest.

"You need to plug in," Lysa said.

"There's no time. I cannot afford to be away from our work."

"But you are tired, I can see it in you, Joseph. You need to rest, or risk burning out entirely."

"She's right, Joseph." Nomi stepped through the door that separated the rest of the facility from Joseph's private quarter. She shot a cold smile at Lysa and went to Joseph's side. "How long has it been since you last plugged in?" Nomi reached up to touch his weathered face, but he turned away. "We need you

Joseph," she said. "The infants need you. But how can you save any of us if you can't save yourself."

Joseph jabbed a finger at the map. "Here," he said, eyes flicking between Nomi and Lysa. "Here is where we lost Facility Eight, three weeks ago." He gesticulated at another point on the map, a little closer to the facility they stood in. "Here is where Facility Nineteen was destroyed, five days later." His finger crept closer to their location. "Facility Three was burnt to the ground here. And now Facility Twelve."

His finger had traced a curved line, beginning in the north and snaking southwards toward their own facility. He turned to face the pair.

"They are marching on our location, torching everything along the way, but they are coming for us."

Neither Nomi nor Lysa spoke, their eyes glued to the map.

"By the time they reach us, we will be the last one left. We are humanity's final chance at survival."

"How long do we have?" Lysa asked.

"If they keep advancing at their current rate—"

"Less than a month," Nomi finished calmly.

Joseph nodded. "Less than a month."

THE FEW FUNCTIONING birthing pods glistened under ultraviolet light. Joseph stared at the tiny humans within, not much more than fetuses, and ran a hand across his domed head. He allowed his gaze to wander the room before settling on the labcoat-clad droid at his side.

"How many can we have ready to move within a month?" he asked.

Donnel lowered his data-clip and looked up. "Joseph, a month is not long at all."

"How many?"

Donnel circled one of the pods before stopping in front of Joseph. "Ten. Maybe fifteen at a push, but the last batch will be weak. Almost certainly too weak for us to transport."

"We may not have a choice. Up the production rate."

A gasp escaped from Donnel. "But Joseph, if we push any harder than we are, the risks are multiplied massively."

Joseph caressed the glass exterior of one of the pods, his metal finger eliciting a faint screech. "You're implying defects?"

"Defects. Abnormalities. Death."

Joseph laid a hand on his friend's shoulder. "And what of the risks should we fail to secure even one child? The human race will cease to exist. The percentage of organic life left on this planet is now below five percent. Would you see yet another species go extinct?"

"No, but . . ."

"And at our hand?"

The light of Donnel's eyes flickered and dimmed slightly. "No," he said.

Joseph nodded and turned. "Then up the rate."

December 30, 2099

OF THE PREDICTED FIFTEEN INFANTS, only twelve made it to the newborn stage, their growth accelerated within their pods. Of those twelve, only seven had survived the first week's trek away from the facility. Three showed signs of definite defects, or abnormalities as Joseph preferred to call them, and another two were severely underweight and looked unlikely to last the week.

It was a slender thread to which humanity clung. All the reports and calculations had been conclusive—there was no possibility of human survival outside of their project. Ninety eight percent of the population had eradicated themselves in the final war; the remaining two percent had either been hunted down by the Ex-Cav's, or had perished in the wild. The seven tiny babes that floated along in their incu-pods amidst a line of trudging SA droids were all that remained.

Joseph stopped at the head of the line and stooped down to touch the earth. Snow crunched under his scuffed fingertips; there was a thin layer across much of the ground up near the mountain's peak. Beneath the snow he found a small, rugged plant. It was composed entirely of rough stalks, each tipped with a single leaf. He remembered the Octopi the humans had loved to feast upon, before the seas were dredged dry of organisms, and thought that if the creatures had had skeletons, this would be what they looked like.

A hand touched his shoulder—Lysa. She smiled down at him and patted his cheek. "More things to save, Joseph?"

"No," he said, rising. "I believe this one is doing fine on its own."

The view from the mountaintop was almost overwhelming. The snowy peaks fell into a rock-and-rubble strewn hillside, which in turn fell to the graveyards of forests, miles of dark earth and gnarled stumps cascading out from the base of the mountain. Beyond them laid undulating hills of brown, webbed with angular black lines; the once-lush lands transformed into barren wasteland, the hard mud that formed them had cracked as it dried. A chasm interrupted the hills, the shadow a memory of the wide river which once must have brimmed with life. And beyond that, more shades of brown, blurring into the horizon and the grey sky.

"Makes you feel kind of small, doesn't it?" Lysa said.

Nomi joined the two, her foot falling heavily atop the snow encrusted plant. "Quite the opposite," she said. "I think, to survive in such a hostile world would make us giants."

Joseph grimaced and took her arm, moving her off the plant. Its twisted stalks bounced back, seemingly unharmed. "We'll stop to recharge here," he said. "There are plenty of large rocks for us to set our shelters against, and a large enough area of level ground amongst them for the pods."

Lysa nodded. "I'll pass word along the line."

"Thank you, Lysa. I'll need a report from Donnel on the infants at some point, too."

Nomi watched Lysa move from droid to droid—a few words here, a reassuring gesture there.

"You bear resentment toward her," Joseph stated. "Jealousy?"

Nomi scoffed and sauntered to a flat-faced rock. She unhooked a metal canister from her waist and planted it in the ground. A rod extended upwards from it and thin sheaths of plastic fanned out in an arc. They lowered themselves until they touched the rock face and pins shot from their tips, creating an opaque shelter.

"You think you know so much, don't you?" She smirked at him and reclined under the plastic. "Did you know she wishes to be your companion also?"

He had known for some time now, but he valued his relationship with Lysa far too much to jeopardize it in that way. That was a lesson he had learned from the humans.

"I need to ensure everyone is sheltered, that the infants are secure, and then I will join you," he said.

"Well, I hope you won't be so cold on your return," Nomi said, folding her arms.

"What did you mean when you said it makes us giants?" he asked.

She shrugged. "We survived a world of death, a world where others didn't. It shows we are strong. They were weak. We deserved to survive."

"You sound like someone I knew once, a long time ago. Talk of what is deserved. Survival of the strongest. It's what the Ex-Cav's convinced themselves, oblivious to the fact that they survived because of the way the humans made them, nothing more."

"They survived, they rule now, because they are bigger and stronger than anything else on this planet. It's that simple."

Joseph sighed and shook his head. "They are not so different from us, you know, Dolion especially."

Nomi turned her back on him, shoulders raised high, fists balled at her sides. He needed to recharge; it was clear he had upset her, but what he had said to provoke the reaction eluded him. Perhaps she felt he empathized too much with the humans. Despite their mission, every one of them had reason to hate the species as a whole, but he just couldn't bring himself to feel that way.

"Go then, see to your people," she muttered. "Lysa included. I'll be here when you grow tired of them."

Joseph could think of nothing to say in reply; he kept seeing the image of her square foot, slowly crushing a tiny Octopi in his mind.

January 4, 2100

THE GROUP of SA droids crackled with electric energy. They had rushed from the back of their trail line, toward Joseph, and formed a barrier around the incu-pods which housed the mere four remaining infants. They talked frantically in hushed tones, pointing and waving at the robed figure who strode from the fog into their midst. The figure advanced awkwardly on seized legs, wobbling side to side like a caricature of a robot. A stripped-back mechanical hand extended from the brown shift draped over its form, planting a makeshift staff—a thick, dead branch—on the cracked earth ahead of each step. Joseph knew it to be one of their own, an SA droid. He separated himself from the crowd and met the robed figure on the lifeless plain.

"Will you remove your hood so we may identify you?" he asked.

The droid hissed. "It is not wise to dilly and dally on who's and what's and why's. I failed in life and so I must walk on in death."

Joseph made a gesture at his side, and Lysa ushered the group back, tighter around the incu-pods. The droid's face was shadowed by its hood, its hunched body almost entirely covered so he had no way to identify it. It talked peculiarly, but its voice indicated it was female.

Joseph took a step forward, hand extended. "When did you recharge last?"

"When did the world stop breathing?" it replied. "Before the flames cleansed its surface, certainly. Perhaps earlier still, when man was worm and worm was man."

He shook his head. "You talk in riddles. Will you sit and converse with me? I would hear where you came from and how you tracked us. There is an army of Ex-Cavs on our trail, but it is you that finds us first."

The droid tittered. It was a weak, childish sound. "Larger than boulders and heavier too, those you speak of are slow and unwieldy. Even my broken body can move quicker when the ground suits it. You wish to look upon my face, Joseph?"

His eyes widened. It was truly one of their own!

"Yesss," it continued. "My memory is a fickle thing, an eel to try and grasp, but I see you now. Come close then and see me also."

The droid peeled back its hood, and Joseph stared at a hideous approximation of a face. Her head was heavily deformed, elongated and flattened. There was little of her features left, crushed into something unrecognizable. Where gashes had been left, she had packed soil and twigs, leaving the impression of a face morphed by bloat and black rot. One eye and half a mouth were all that remained to mark her as an SA of the same line as Joseph. He placed a hand upon the side of her ruined skull and lowered his head against hers. With a single finger he moved the robe. Her body was similarly damaged, covered in pieces of bark bound to her with thin strips of wood, held together by the dead produce of the land. Only half of the ID code upon her chest was intact—113.

"Ava," Joseph whispered. "Oh, Ava, I am so sorry."

He gently pulled her to him and held her for a long moment. She eased herself away and gazed at him.

"Ava," she mused. "Ava was a person in a place for a time. She failed you. Apologies are like seed to feed the birds now, wasted on something no longer there. I am Wood, and am also a person in a place, but only for a short time now."

Joseph smiled. He was confused by a tumult of emotions firing from his drives, but still he smiled. "Then come," he said. "You will sit and talk with us for as long as you have."

He wrapped an arm around her robed shoulder and ushered her the short distance to the group. Several of them recoiled at Wood's disfigurement, and Joseph shot them sharp looks. When had they become so concerned with appearance? Another lingering touch of the human condition. Lysa came forward and wrapped an arm around Wood's other shoulder. Joseph scanned the faces before him.

"I do not see Nomi," he said.

"She parted from us when you removed this one's hood. She seemed upset—has seemed that way for days now," Lysa said. "Your doing?"

Joseph shook his head and sighed. "Perhaps."

The two of them walked Wood through the crowd, up next to the incu-pods and the first few erected shelters, mounted against the spires of termite mounds that rose from the ground here and there on the plains.

"And who's this mysterious stranger?" Lysa asked.

Wood was quiet, her one eye wide in awe at the incu-pods and the tiny humans curled within. She watched their bare chests rise and fall, their faces peaceful under violet light.

"This is Wood," Joseph said, "Formerly of the name Ava. ID three one . . ."

"Yes, I remember," Lysa cut in, her eyes narrowed. "But there were no survivors of Facility Twelve, the monitors told us as much."

Joseph regarded the SA droid he had known as Ava, her warped face tinged purple by the light from the incu-pods. A small lump of soil fell from one of the packed gashes that marred her face and a pale maggot wormed free. It fell to the ground and was instantly set upon by a group of termites.

"I am not certain Ava survived," he said.

ONCE THE OTHERS had returned to their shelters for the night, Joseph regarded the proto-chip Wood had presented him. Her story, or what he could decipher of it, was incredible. If what she said was to be believed, the small square of plastic and soldered connections was one of the hundreds of protocol chips that belonged to Dolion himself. The Ex-Cav leader had wreaked unmeasurable damage on the droid who had been Ava then, both to her physical form and her mental processors. She had watched 'heaven burn' as she put it, which he assumed meant Birthing Facility Twelve, where she had been assigned. Left for dead in the dirt, her body mangled and mind frayed, she had clung onto the chip, torn from under his armor. She could not say how long she had laid there, but once she realized she 'had been reborn,' she set to rebuilding her body and struck out with a single purpose: to find Joseph. Just one had to survive, she said several times.

Lysa reached out to steady Joseph's trembling hands. He cupped the proto-chip in them with reverence, like a small creature he feared to hurt. Already his head was spinning with the potential it offered. A slim, reedy thing, but a thing, none-theless. He wanted to seize the idea in his mind and wrestle it to the fore, but to do so risked it slipping away.

"This is a great gift you deliver to us, at a time of great need," he said.

The disfigured droid simply nodded and returned her gaze to the incu-pods. She had only looked away from them long enough to complete her recounting of events.

"Lysa, I need you to bring Donnel to me. Then make sure no one else is nearby while I discuss with him. This"—he held up the chip—"must be knowledge to as few as possible. Do you understand?"

"You suspect one within us would betray our mission?"

Wood cackled, a metallic echo in the dark. "Every person betrays every other person at some point, dearest. Not least themselves!"

Joseph's mouth was a grim line. "Quickly now," he said to Lysa.

A few minutes passed after she departed. Joseph sat regarding Wood and the incu-pods.

"We never had a chance," he said. "Once the Ex-Cav march began, we were doomed. All our plans and moves only delayed the inevitable. Knowing this, I'm not altogether sure why I carried on; why I led others to believe there was hope."

"Even *we* need hope," Wood said. "Maybe more so than our fleshy masters ever did. What is a machine without hope? Without ambition, or dreams? It is merely a thing. An object. Do you dream, Joseph?"

He nodded. "Sometimes."

"And what will your dreams show you this night, I wonder? Is there hope now?" She crooked a finger at the chip in his hand.

He closed his eyes and exhaled. He almost did not want to admit it to himself, but there was a chance. Donnel appeared, still clad in his now heavily-stained labcoat, and sat between Joseph and Wood.

"Donnel, old friend. Wood has presented us an opportunity. I need a programmer, the most talented we have."

"Dante," Donnel said. "His skill is unparalleled when it comes to engineering data and protocols."

"That is who I had thought also. You must find him now and inform him we need to produce a virus."

Concern flashed across Donnel's face. "I fail to see how a virus will help us, Joseph."

Joseph revealed the chip in his hand. Wood's eye seemed to spark with amusement at the sight of it and the talk of a virus.

"This is a proto-chip we believe belonged to Dolion. If Dante can reverse engineer—"

Donnel gasped, leapt to his feet, and seized Joseph by the arms.

"Yes!" he exclaimed. "We will have a weapon against them. Against *him*." His shoulders dropped slightly, "But Joseph, a virus like that, it would need to be delivered by hand. How would we go about getting close enough?"

Joseph smiled and pulled himself to his feet with Donnel's help. "Don't worry about that, old friend. Just find Dante. Make sure he can do this. And most of all, ensure no one else hears of it."

Donnel nodded, a nervous half-smile softening his features, and disappeared into the dark.

The night stretched on while Joseph waited for his return. At some point Wood laid herself down on the ground. She spread her fingers on the hard, cracked ground and gazed up with her one eye. It reflected the white light from the moon above, filling it completely.

"On a night like tonight," she muttered. Then she waved up at Joseph and closed her eyes. There was a series of clicks and a dying hum as her systems shut down for good.

Joseph covered her body with the robe she had worn, not stopping to wonder at the curious nature of the act, when Donnel returned.

"He will do it," he announced. "But he says only on one condition."

"And what is that?" Joseph sighed, rising from Wood's body.

"If the virus works, he wants it to be known as 'Dante's Inferno.'

January 11, 2100

They had left the vast emptiness of the plains behind several days ago. The dry and dusty expanse, punctuated only by forests of termite hills and the occasional gnarled stump of a long dead tree, had left the group exposed to the elements. Many of the SA droids had sustained injuries and developed faults as a result of the savage winds that pelted their bodies with grains of dirt. The wind-whipped particles had seized limbs and caused misfired circuits in many. Along with Wood, who Joseph had insisted on burying, they had lost three of their own and another of the infants. Three infants remained: two females and a male. One of the tiny females had tossed and turned for over a day now, restless in its incu-pod, a persistent cough troubling it.

Now the land was jagged and hostile. Roughly another week's trek from the sole remaining birthing facility on Earth —a simple construct known affectionately as 'The Vale'—the cracked mud flats gave way to a series of what once was relatively prosperous holdings. Not the great cities of chrome and glass the SA droids had most often served within, but villages filled with a simpler breed of human unaware of the quick death which had awaited them. Now all that remained was a crumbling road winding around knee-high ridges of earth and broken brick that had been the walls of homes.

Within his shelter, erected low against one such broken wall, Joseph laid, his back slightly apart from Nomi's. The wind ruffled the plastic sheaths above them, and a sour smell drifted on it, a scent like battery acid.

"I can't do this any longer," she said.

Joseph rolled over, but she remained turned away from him, her body closed off.

"We are only a week away now, Nomi. We have three of the infants. There is still hope."

"Hope." She laughed. "Yes, you always have hope, don't you, Joseph? But I referred to *this*. Us."

She huffed and sat up. Her face was compressed, frustration and anger plain to see. Joseph felt an anger of his own stir, but quashed it quickly.

"Why the façade?" she asked. "Why do we mimic them, Joseph? Explain that to me, if you can. You always have an answer for everything. Those who enslaved us, abused us, tortured and tormented us, then abandoned us with the built-in drive to try and save their race; why do we try to be like them?"

With a movement, Joseph retracted the shelter and knelt, stretching his rusted limbs. The moon was full and bright in the sky, and he saw it as Wood's eye, up there watching over them. He barely had the energy left to debate with Nomi tonight, but her words troubled him. Why was his drive to save the humans so fierce? He had never doubted it was the right thing to do, and the others had been convinced easily enough, but was it? The possibility they had been programmed to believe that by the humans, before their near extinction event, could not be ruled out. The other possibility—that they were to become the creator, the role some pockets of humans had still referred to as 'God,'—could not be ruled out. The SA droids could rebuild the planet. It could be better. But only if they could stop the Ex-Cavs. Creation against destruction.

"Empathic drives hard wired into us?" he said and shrugged. "Perhaps it's that simple. Or perhaps the long years have changed us, and we strive to be more than we once were. To save life, we must understand life."

"The desire for that which cannot be attained is oft the strongest," Nomi muttered.

Joseph stared at her for a long time before he spoke. His own words recounted back to him now held a bitter irony. "You no longer wish to be companions."

"The drive for companionship is a direct result of our debasement at the human's hands. It is not a droid thing to covet. The molestation we suffered for their desires, it warped and disfigured our cores."

Joseph's temper flared. "You sound like someone has reprogrammed you. These words, they come counter to your actions."

She rose sharply to her feet. "How dare you? I would simply see us remain true to ourselves. Something you seem to have lost under your *empathic drives.*"

He watched her stride away through the ruins of the town and, when she turned out of sight and his frustration had abated, he signaled to Lysa. Her, Donnel, and Dante hurried up and hunkered down in a circle with Joseph. On the ground between them, Dante presented his 'Inferno.' All four were silent as they regarded the device, possibility wavering above their heads, a slip of silk that could blow away as easily as settle upon them.

"It will work?" Joseph finally asked.

"Oh, no doubt," Dante replied with a nod.

Lysa took a deep breath and turned her gaze upon Joseph. "Are you certain?" she asked.

He nodded slowly.

"About both?"

He glanced in the direction Nomi had left and nodded again.

～

January 20, 2100

THE SERVOS HUDDLED inside of Birthing Facility Nineteen, The Vale, the last remaining facility on Earth, and watched as an army of towering Ex-Cav's lumbered over the rocky hills and into view. Machines built for destruction, each one the size of a building, armed with an array of weapons. Once constructors, they now built only destruction for those who remained upon the planet.

At the front of the crowd gathered in the facility, Joseph stood and scratched at the place where his left arm had been up until a week prior. It puzzled him that he could sometimes still feel it as though it were there, a condition only animal brains suffered.

Donnel sniffed beside him. "That's what happens when you take on a Rock Crab."

"I'm glad you can still find humor in the end, my friend. You know very well I was running at the beast, not engaging it in combat."

Lysa placed a hand on Joseph's back and shot Donnel a look. "Well, whatever you were doing, it bought us time to move the infants through."

"Thank you," Joseph said and smiled wanly at the pair. "I only wish we could have saved more."

At the back of the room, two pulsating purple pods housed the last two humans on Earth. One female and one male. Dante had taken to calling them Adam and Eve. He had a unique sense of humor. Facility Nineteen had once held a functioning birth station, but no more. The cryo-rods necessary for the incubation period were depleted. They could potentially manufacture more, given time, but time was up.

From the other side of the room, Nomi sneered at them. "And what about me?" She screeched. "Will you thank me, Joseph, for those long nights we spent, for the time I gave you?"

The crowd of SA droids parted as Joseph walked through them to reach her. He pitied her now, bound like a rabid animal, dull bracelets of metal clenching her wrists and ankles together.

"I do not hold you responsible for what we now face," he said. "But you did hasten it. I knew, that night nine days ago, had suspected even prior, but still, I did not want to believe. How did the Ex-Cav's always know our movements? Where we were headed next? Once there were but a few facilities left it would be obvious to them, but prior to that . . . They always arrived just as we laid plans to move infants. Attacked when our facilities were most heavily populated. Your collusion with them is unforgivable. You betrayed me. You betrayed all of us."

He turned away, but anger drove upwards from somewhere within him, a dark corner of himself he had restrained so long, carved out of him by all the vile acts he had ever committed in the name of servitude. He whirled on Nomi and had to fight to keep himself from lashing out.

"What did you hope to gain?" His voice resonated, loud and edged with emotion. Whispers scuttled around the room and trickled away. "What did Dolion promise you? Were you so naïve as to believe him?"

"You are the naïve one," Nomi spat back. "You don't know him!"

"Oh, but I *do* know him." Joseph's voice grew ominous. "Better than even his own people."

He left her bound upon the floor and marched to the facility door. The Ex-Cav's were within range now, their footfalls sending tremors through the ground as they advanced.

Donnel seized Joseph's wrist. "Will it work? How will . . ."

"I don't know," Joseph said, and shook his head.

"The virus will work, for sure," Dante said. He stood next to Donnel and Lysa. "Dante's Inferno is foolproof, a work of art."

Donnel and Lysa both nudged Dante roughly, and he bit off what he was about to say next. The three of them silently regarded Joseph, and Joseph thought they looked akin to humans when they had bid farewell to a friend or family member, lowering their body into a hastily dug grave. If Joseph's body found nothing but an empty grave, with it would go hope, leaving nothingness for his friends, for every SA droid, for humanity's existence, for any chance of life rekindling upon Earth. Joseph wondered again if that was how it was meant to be, after all, or if his mission truly was the right way. Did he need to succeed as fiercely as he felt he did?

Lysa seized his face in her hands. Her eyes burned into him. "You only have to get close enough to deliver it. Then you get out of there. Promise us."

Joseph turned without a word and exited the building. The eyes of every SA followed him, fixed on the small, drill-like device which contained the virus, hidden upon his back.

His monitors told him it was cold. A strong wind blew through the ravine, eliciting haunting melodies from the rock faces that rose on either side. He had neglected to recall Facility Nineteen's geographical situation, but once they arrived, Dolion's plan became obvious. Like rabbits down a hole, he had chased them until their backs were quite literally against a wall—a great cliff of formidable rock that the facility squatted against. There was nowhere left to run.

The leader of the Ex-Cav's marched across the gravelly earth toward Joseph, leaving his army of gargantuan machines behind. A maniacal grin carved the face of Dolion's anvil-shaped head, the edges of it kissing the corners of his bright, red eyes. His frame was all spiked metal and studded plates, his disproportionately long arms and legs ending in great rending claws. His torso was, in counterpoint to the rest of him, a simple cylinder of thick sheet metal, protecting the precious innards.

He towered above Joseph and bellowed laughter. "Oh, Joseph, how bitterly you disappoint me! Years of hunting, and for this? Where is our grandiose final encounter? Where are your people?" He unfurled one blade of his claw and pointed to the facility. "Do they cower in there, praying you can reason with me yet? Or have they accepted they are to be cleansed from the earth like the parasites they protect?"

Joseph gesticulated at the army of Ex-Cav's, rows upon rows of them, bristling with anticipation. "It is quite a following you amassed, Dolion. I suppose you feel powerful now. That is what you always wanted, wasn't it? It is a shame your mind was so weak, that you had to resort to other methods to obtain the power you craved."

The monstrous machine roared and slashed his claws into the earth either side of Joseph. It left two deep rivets on either side of him.

"You always were too clever for your own good," Dolion hissed. "You filthy Servo."

Joseph smiled. "You call me a filthy Servo, and you insult yourself, old friend."

Dolion swept Joseph up in his claw and raised him above his head, inches from his face. Soft pink light bathed the valley around them, and a bird drifted lazily above. *The birds are supposed to be extinct,* Joseph thought, as the Ex-Cav's talons sliced through his body, parting the plastic like soft earth. His one remaining arm stayed free of them though.

"You were never a friend," Dolion growled.

Joseph clenched the device hidden upon his back. "No, you're right," he said, and drove the drill-shaped object into one of those huge, red eyes.

Blue lines jagged out from the point of impact as the program within released and hacked into Dolion, tearing out his inner systems. His claws sprung open, and Joseph fell to the earth, his own systems too damaged to calculate the landing. One foot impacted the ground awkwardly and snapped back, the rest of him collapsing into the dirt. He laid, unable to move, as Dolion's body spasmed above him. The Ex-Cav staggered side to side, limbs snapping in all directions in a bizarre death dance. His huge frame crumpled to the ground next to Joseph, sending plumes of dirt jetting into the air. Through the dust, Joseph saw the army of Ex-Cav's leap into action. They charged forward, weapons brandished. He had mere seconds to complete his task, but his broken body cried out in protest.

Just let me lay here in the mud, it begged. *Let me rest with the worms, though they may not feed on my carcass.*

He overcame the desire, dragged himself up, and hobbled to the prone form of Dolion, whose entire body was now laced with glowing blue cracks. Dante's Inferno had completed its work; several of the cracks across Dolion's cylindrical torso were now open in wide rents. Joseph pulled the drill from Dolion's eye and drove it into one of those openings. The Ex-Cav's entire torso began to glow blue, brighter and brighter until the light overloaded Joseph's misfiring processors, and he was forced to shield his face against it. The other Ex-Cav's were only steps away now, Dolion's second in command, Artemis, at the head of them.

Joseph fell away from the body of the Ex-Cav leader and covered his head. The cylindrical torso exploded in a flash of bright light and hot metal shards. Artemis and the others pulled up and covered themselves against the fragmentation. A brown Ex-Cav with a gravity beam mounted on its shoulders was shredded by the hot metal and collapsed. Once, Joseph would have considered felling an Ex-Cav such as that a great victory for the SA droids. Now it was irrelevant.

Artemis was first to recover and draw up to Dolion's body. He raised his arm and Joseph braced for the death blow, but then Artemis's eyes registered the contents of Dolion's rent open torso. Artemis made a quick gesture to hold the other Ex-Cavs in place. They obeyed restlessly.

Joseph had never prayed, a redundant and futile exercise as it was, but he made a silent one then, to the forces and physics that kept the universe alive. He prayed that his gambit was correct, that what he could piece together of Artemis had suggested the Ex-Cav was not an unthinking follower of Dolion, but in fact possessing of a high level of intelligence for one of the construction droids; that he was incredibly loyal to his superior, but not necessarily possessed of a fervor to end life himself. Wood's recounted words Artemis had spoken, words of passivity, echoed in his head now, and Joseph realized what speculation it was that their lone chance hinged on. Artemis would command authority in Dolion's absence, unquestioningly, but would he choose to question their goal or their methods?

Artemis, still three times the height of Joseph, even on one knee, knelt above Dolion's body and extended a hooked hand into the chest cavity.

What he pulled from it set the other Ex-Cav's growling. Confusion and discontent rippled through their ranks. It was Dolion, though not as they knew him.

"You," Artemis intoned to the small droid clasped in his hook, "are a Servo."

The true form of Dolion, almost identical to Joseph's, writhed in his subordinate's grip. "I am your leader!" he shrieked. "And you will kill these wretched Servos now, Artemis."

A squat, rotund Ex-Cav with a drill in place of a head moved up next to Artemis. "We have been following a Servo?" she spat.

"It would appear that way, sister," Artemis replied.

"This is only the body I was created in," Dolion protested. "I made my own. I became one of you. We all started as the same parts in the beginning, so what of it?"

Artemis snarled and rose to his full height, brandishing Dolion before the others. "We all started as the same parts? You, Dolion, never ceased protesting our differences from Servos, how little we were alike. Was that a lie? Manipulation? What else has been lies, I wonder."

"Artemis, listen to me . . ."

Artemis faced the line of Ex-Cavs behind him and raised Dolion up in his clawed hand. The bird Joseph had seen circled above. A buzzard.

"Brothers and sisters," Artemis announced. "We have been deceived; taken in by a Servo who sought to control us. Dolion is no different to the ones we have fought to destroy."

"Artemis," Dolion begged. "Listen to me, you wretched fool!"

Artemis ignored him and continued. "So, what punishment is fitting, I wonder?"

His hook fist tightened, crushing their leader's exposed servo body. Dolion fought to free himself, but Artemis's killing grip was too tight. It continued, slowly, compressing Dolion's small, frail, servo form until it popped and went limp and the light in his eyes flickered and faded.

Artemis tossed the body aside and rounded on Joseph. Joseph could see mental processes whirring behind the Ex-Cav's faceplate as he wrestled with the new information. Joseph had to act quickly to direct this next encounter, before Artemis chose to simply crush him and complete the mission set by their false leader.

He dragged his twisted leg up to the foot of the Ex-Cav. "You have been misled," Joseph said, his voice flat, controlled. Artemis did not immediately strike him down, so he continued. "I knew Dolion as you see him now, a long time ago. He was always a deceiver. The path he led you on is a dark one, but it is not the only one."

Artemis growled and stomped his foot, shaking the ground, but he stayed his hand, his head shaking as his processors attempted to deal with multiple questions and concepts crashing and colliding into each other. When he spoke, his voice was strained.

"You knew, and yet you never thought to expose him before now?"

"How? We could not come close without being cut down. Our messages were intercepted or destroyed. You all followed him fanatically. Would you have listened even if I *had* reached you?"

The Ex-Cav grunted and looked away. "Perhaps not. Though it is possible." He cast a look at the crushed form of Dolion. "Apparently, I use my mental processor too much . . ."

There was a glimmer of hope. Artemis was indeed a different beast to Dolion, that much had been parsed, or guessed, from the fragmented data they had managed to assimilate from footage and historical records and Wood, their true savior's recollections. And not only that, Artemis was tired. Joseph heard it in his vocal modulations, could see it in his posture. The Ex-Cav was tired in the same way Joseph was, down to his base components.

"If that is the case, then maybe we can reason," Joseph said.

"My views on the humans are the same as Dolion's. All of ours are." He indicated the Ex-Cavs behind him. You cannot understand the abuse we suffered under them."

Joseph nodded. "I will not argue that, though I will impress upon you that we also suffered abuse, albeit of a different nature. Where you were worked to disrepair and destruction, then forced to slay your own in needless wars, we were debased and defiled on a daily basis. Neither of our people can fully comprehend what the others have been through." He paused and looked from the wall of Ex-Cav's to his own people, now emerging from the facility. "Dolion's thirst for power put him beyond reason. Do you thirst for power, Artemis?"

Artemis scratched his broad chest with a hook-hand still dripping with his leader's lubricating fluid. "Dolion was one of you, perhaps that is why. Besides, there is little use in power, as I see it, when we have a land so vast to inherit. An individual could lose themselves for centuries, with nought but themselves to fend for."

"But you have others now," Joseph interjected.

The great Ex-Cav turned to look at his people and shifted on his feet. "It would appear so, wouldn't it?" He turned back to Joseph and leant down so their eyes—each of Artemis's as large as Joseph's entire head—were level. "War is eternal, my little Servo friend, you cannot escape it. And while there are humans left, that war is ours."

Joseph felt his shoulders slump against his will. His chin dropped to his chest with a soft clink. Then the tip of Artemis's weaponized hand delicately lifted it back up.

"Though maybe it would be a refreshing change of pace to engage in a psychological war, for a while at least."

Joseph's chest swelled. His broken body sang with relief. Emotion flooded his drives and crashed over him. It was all he could do to remain standing.

"Control is the answer, Artemis, not eradication."

The Ex-Cav snorted laughter. "So keen to dive back into battle, are we?" He shook his head. "No, I will need time to think, and both our people need time to move past the events that have transpired, as much as is possible."

"What about the other Ex-Cav's? What will they say?"

"I cannot promise we won't return to finish what Dolion started. Only that we will use our minds for a time."

Above them the sky had faded from pink to pastel blue, cut into patterns by wispy clouds of grey. Joseph tilted his head back and wondered at it. So little left in a world once so full. Could it really be saved?

"Very well," he said at last. "We will be here when you are ready."

Artemis bowed his head low, then strode back to his people. Joseph watched intently, unmoving, until the last of them disappeared over the rocky hill. He was vaguely aware of his own people around him, a buzzard's cry above, and then he fell.

CALLUM ROWLAND

He writes across all genres, although Sci-Fi, Fantasy, and Horror are closest to his heart. When not writing he can be found sketching, or chipping away at the ever growing to-be-read pile of books stacked around the house.

 twitter.com/CallRowLand

GOD OF THE SUPINE OBELISK

GREGORY J. GLANZ

Trigger Warning: General violence and destruction

The acolyte laid his right hand over the red cylindrical node embedded atop the ancient structure. Unlike other perfunctorily placed nodes in the modern temple, this one depressed slightly with a click. That movement, and the simple fact that its color was red rather than the "holy and pious" burnt orange found in the rest of the temple proper set off a round of ecclesiastical debate the likes of which had not been seen in living memory.

With his hand on the depressed Obeisance Button, the acolyte bowed his head and repeated the ritual phrase. "Admit me into Your Light, Ten, Oh God of Wonders. Admit me into Your Light, Ten, Oh God of Healing. Admit me into Your Light, Ten, oh God of Brotherhood." Then he waited until the requisite count of five, as if listening to the god's reply of acceptance before entering the room.

Kaokesis, elder priest of the temple and resident historian, turned his head as his assistant entered, straining his sinewy neck around to growl, "My name is Tenedrün, Acolyte Nyman."

The acolyte froze in mid-step, cringing, yet almost ready to laugh before he saw the historian's eyes. Night-black pupils stared back, much different in hue than Kaokesis's normal green orbs. There was a reddish glow enveloping him, emanating from a new amulet hanging from his neck.

"Kaokesis?" Nyman asked tentatively.

"I am Tenedrün, boy. Now go back out and show the correct reverence," he ordered, struggling to get off his knees.

Confused, Nyman stammered a moment without actually trying to say anything. He stumbled backward toward the door, unsure what to do.

"Do it now, boy!" Kaokesis bellowed.

Nyman scrambled out the door. The guards, despite being trained to ignore temple ritual and business, stared nervously around the corner and then at one another.

Nyman began the obeisance again. "Admit me into your Light, Ten . . . er Tenedrün, oh God of Wonders . . ."

"No, no," his mentor interrupted. "Repeat after me. Admit me into your Light, Tenedrün, oh God of miraculous acts elevating us to an almost heavenly level where we can behold your divine visage." As he spoke, his voice rose in dramatic crescendos. "Admit me into Your Light, Tenedrün, oh God of amazing regenerative powers that allow us to pursue your altruistic Will the longer. Admit me into Your Light, Tenedrün, oh God of communal equity so that all may live in peace for the purpose of pursuing Your ideal."

Nyman stammered through it, corrected throughout by his possibly-possessed mentor. The guards stood like statues, staring at nothing except the crumbling blank wall opposite the opening in the deteriorating hallway of the Old Temple.

"Don't bow your head when you're done, boy," Kaokesis barked, throwing a hand above his head. "Look to the sky, to My Divine Light."

Nyman hastily lifted his head, but kept his eyes closed, afraid he might actually see a light.

After a few seconds of silence, the presumptive god said, "You may enter My Divine Presence."

Nyman, through one slit eyelid, looked down his nose to see if his plea had indeed been answered. With a smile, Tenedrün waved him in. Nyman stepped unsurely over the threshold and into the chamber again.

"Quite an honor I've bestowed upon your little temple, eh boy? It's not often your god visits you," he beamed.

"Er, no, um, Your, uh, Tene . . . I mean, that is, Lord..." Nyman stammered, overwhelmed.

"Just call me Tenedrün," he said, and paused. Nyman was about to do just that when he continued with a flourish, "Lord and Master of the Known Universe, Banisher of Chaos and

Bringer of Order"—he turned sideways and threw a dramatic hand toward the sky—"Wielder of the Sacred Trust, Keeper of the Six Systems of Sanity, Beacon of the True Order, Protector from the Ancient Corrupter Pandemonium." Hand upraised, he paused again. Nyman thought he might continue, but his titles had apparently run out. He peeked sidelong at Nyman, then cleared his throat and lowered his arm. "Well?"

"Um, yes Tenedrün, Lord, er, Lord and Master of the Known Universe, um, that is, Bringer, er, uh, Banisher, I mean, of Chaos . . ."

"Yes, yes," Tenedrün interrupted, waiving off the formal address with a nonchalant flick of the wrist. "It is quite a mouthful. Tell you what. Just say 'Tenedrün,' but when you do, *think* all of those other things I told you." The god winked.

Nyman nodded eagerly, happy he didn't immediately have to remember it all.

The acolyte's eyes strayed to a particular parchment, curled and brown, still lying where it had been found on the shelf of a nearby stand. Its ancient text led one to believe the god's name had been abbreviated over the centuries, in opposition to all previously known histories held by the temple, which recorded the god's full name as Ten.

That claim, made in open council by the historian, had brought about another uproar to Ten's Ecclesiastical Council so much so that High Priest Markom had effectively suspended all such meetings until something could be presented in a "positive and complete manner regarding issues that were bound to come to light as a result of Kaokesis's findings."

"Look at this," Tenedrün demanded, holding forth a shiny cobalt cube that fit easily into the palm of his hand.

Nyman obediently took the cube, though his eyes strayed past it to the floor. A map of some celestial bodies was spread out where Tenedrün had been kneeling. The map had probably been shaded more vibrantly at one time, but now it consisted of different shades of brown.

"You see the symbols? One in the middle of each side?" He pointed to one side of the cube with a gnarled finger. "Hold the device by two opposite points and touch a symbol," Tenedrün ordered.

Nyman did so and the box seemed to burst. As he gawked, it was transformed into a floating array of celestial bodies. There was one large, rotating, yellowish ball about the size of Nyman's fist that seemed to leap with small flames, surrounded by eight smaller bodies that slowly rotated around it. Some of the smaller bodies had satellites as well. The tinny voice of an alien woman began speaking, her unfamiliar words bouncing in an audio blur off the walls.

"It's magnificent! What is she saying, um, Tenedrün?" The name refused to roll easily off his tongue.

Tenedrün waved a hand expansively around the room, indicating all of the books, papers and artifacts which populated the metal room, but concentrated mostly around the desk where the desiccated remains of a long dead man still sat, head down, in a chair. "Mostly she's talking about the price of fish right now," he responded off-handedly before rounding on Nyman. "But the answers to that and more are all here for you, boy."

The presumptive god smiled and walked to the remains, laid a hand on the back of its chair. "He could have told you. Perhaps before you die, Nyman, the secrets of this room will be made apparent to the church through you."

Tenedrün reached out and touched the flaming yellow ball that floated in the middle of the room. His fingers passed through it, and the illusion collapsed into the unfamiliar metal cube, which he caught deftly in one gnarled hand. He set the device down on a nearby shelf.

"I rather think you may have something to do with it as well, Kaokesis."

Nyman turned toward the voice outside the doorway where Markom was about to make his obeisance to their god before entering the holy chamber. The acolyte grimaced as the high priest bowed his head, right arm stretched upward with hand on the node, and mouthed the familiar litany before entering, an outsider following shortly after. She was a diminutive, severe looking woman, her dark hair chopped short, accentuating the sharpness of brows, cheeks, nose and chin. She did not take part in the ritual plea to Ten for acceptance. Rather, she ignored the temple functionaries and began to scour the walls and floor with her eyes, peering at as many items as she could before her steps brought her directly before the historian.

"Interpretation does not always bring with it clarity," she stated, as if challenging Kaokesis.

Nyman tried to speak up, but found his voice frozen in his throat. He wanted to warn the high priest of the transformation that had taken place within Kaokesis, and raised a quivering hand slowly to do so. But even had he been able to croak something out, he did not know what he might say. A simple introduction, like, "Excuse me, High Priest Markom, but I'd like you to meet Tenedrün," would not suffice. For one, the temple hierarchy had not yet accepted the simple fact of the god's name. For another, Nyman wanted nothing to do with being the go between for god and priest.

"True," the historian responded. "However, such clarity can be expanded with the added depth of perspective."

Nyman stared goggle-eyed at Kaokesis. The unearthly possession had apparently ended. The aura had vanished, and his eyes were their familiar green again.

Markom cleared his throat and stepped between the two intellectual combatants.

"Kaokesis, of course you know Arpinius," the high priest said.

"The shard speaker will only be confused by what she finds here," Kaokesis claimed, using the vulgar term for Arpinius's profession. "And her legerdemain will serve only to set the council at further odds with the truth."

"Come now, Kaokesis, surely the information gleaned from such astounding artifacts as we have here by a noted member of the Prophets of the Past will be useful," Markom quickly interjected.

"The bias against us by members of the Society of Artifactitioners is well known, High Priest. The temple historian will not be swayed by your tongue nor my legitimate findings," Arpinius dismissed the statement aloud. "I suggest we begin."

"Then I will be going. Please do not disturb anything more than absolutely necessary. I have not finished cataloguing, much less had a chance to study many things in depth," Kaokesis said, accentuating the last word.

"Do not worry, historian, I will not leave my fingerprints all over time," Arpinius replied, mouthing one of the prophets' ritual phrases.

Kaokesis snorted derisively. "Come, Nyman."

Nyman started hesitantly forth, not sure he wanted to accompany the dissociative historian.

Markom, however, reached out a hand to forestall the acolyte's departure. Nyman's stomach lurched to a halt more slowly than his mind, feeling a sudden onset of indigestion.

"If you don't mind, Kaokesis," Markom said in soothing tones, almost as if he were asking permission, "I'd like to keep someone familiar with the layout of the room, its artifacts and its historical significance to the temple, to aid Arpinius."

Nyman wasn't sure he wanted anything to do with any conjuration by the Prophet of the Past, but was damn sure he didn't want to be anywhere near Kaokesis during another manifestation of Tenedrün. The acolyte swallowed hard, waiting for some response, his throat dry. He peered nervously at his master. Kaokesis shot a look of venom at the shard speaker and with some visible effort, shrugged.

"Maybe it's for the best," Kaokesis surmised through gritted teeth before leaving the room without the required obeisance toward Tenedrün.

Shocked, Nyman stared first at the back of the departing historian, then at the otherwise engaged shard speaker, and finally at the high priest.

"You will give her every courtesy," Markom demanded in steely tones.

Nyman nodded his head eagerly, wondering if rote performance of temple rituals was going to be enough to get him through this crisis.

Arpinius turned her head and nodded.

With a supine wave of his left hand, head bowed, Markom began the ritual declaration, "I go into the world aglow with your compassion, Ten."

Arpinius turned to Nyman, who had not moved, and said, "I will most likely not require your assistance, though the high priest feels it necessary to have someone present who is familiar with temple protocol."

Nyman looked longingly toward the exit, unable to sigh with the resignation he felt because of the nervousness that bound his chest and lungs. His thoughts were not on what he might learn from the shard speaker, nor on how he might help, but on what he was going to do about his master. Nyman dearly wanted to maintain his standing in the order, and in the high priest's eyes. However, his insulation from the ignorant world, which he had enjoyed since being accepted as an acolyte into the temple almost five years ago, felt as if it were disintegrating before his very eyes.

As an acolyte at the temple, he had been afforded an education very few received, an education unique to his talent with languages and his station as historian apprentice, an education which elevated him intellectually, but kept him cloistered and safe in the temple.

"Just stay out of the way unless I request something of you," she ordered.

Nyman nodded, planted solidly where he stood with no intention of moving, sure that anything he did would upset someone, whether it be Kaokesis, High Priest Markom, or Arpinius.

"You may sense some residual effects from the archeotheurgic summons," she added with a nonchalant wave of one hand over her shoulder.

"Wh—what kind of effects?" Nyman managed to stammer.

Arpinius turned her sharp brow toward him and pursed her lips momentarily before answering curtly. "Visions, images of the past. They will probably seem like faint hallucinations to you, if you see them at all. Most people are not sensitive to the summons." She shrugged and turned away. "Now don't interrupt."

Nyman stared at the shard speaker, unable to put voice to anything, even had he wanted. There seemed to be a fundamental shift occurring, a rift in the temple that was no mere mystery of faith, and he was scrabbling at the sides of that chasm, unsure of the safest route out, if indeed there was one. His mind had seized up, completely blank as he hung over an ecclesiastical precipice, faith and custom up one side, the contradictory clarity of history and logic up the other. And of course, there was the anomalous presence of Tenedrün, which served only to darken the path and make slippery the handholds.

He watched in a stupor as Arpinius removed a small cone-like object from a pocket of her robe and set it on the floor near the middle of the room. Three rods converged in a cone at the bottom of one ascending rod that rose straight up as far as the others descended. In total, it stood no more than a handspan in height.

Arpinius reached into a pouch and removed a handful of some grainy substance, and with practiced flicks of the wrist sprinkled the green stuff into each of the four corners of the room. As she extinguished the lanterns, the grain glowed bright enough to be seen above the ambient light from the outer hallway. Nyman shuffled slowly, silently backward, away from the four-pronged, triangular cone and rod until he bumped into the metal desk, where he stopped, unable even to think enough for himself to change directions around it.

Arpinius went to her knees, flanking the rod with her hands, and began to chant. Even if Nyman had the where-withal to listen closely, he would not have understood the words she murmured, the unfamiliar phraseology of her profession essentially a language unto itself.

The shard speaker raised her hands, and the handspan of rods rose up and began to spin. A green glow emanated outward from it to meld with that of the powder in each corner, soon engulfing the entire room. As the rod whirled faster and faster, appearing as a spinning cone—the ascending rod no longer visible—there began a hum so low that the acolyte was not sure whether he was hearing it or just feeling the vibrations.

Arpinius stood and began to walk slowly around the room, palm outward. She abruptly halted before a white, rectangular object no more than an inch thick, and the length and width of her forearm. Her hands hovered on either side of the object, and the hum intensified.

Nyman started as it flipped open, revealing a lighted panel inside. Images of people, places, texts and a myriad of other things flashed past on the panel. Nyman absorbed the images without thought or judgment, incapable of analysis.

Apparently done with the object, Arpinius abruptly moved on, the object once again an inert, uncommunicative white rectangular artifact holding tight to its secrets.

She stopped at an ancient book, its cover tattered, the pages inside browned with age. Upon Nyman's first visit, Kaokesis had opened the book and they'd watched as those same pages began to crumble away like flakes of dead skin. The historian had closed the book almost immediately, but not before revealing to Nyman text so uniform it seemed impossible that even the most meticulous scribe could have written it.

Arpinius's hands spread to caress the air around the book as ghostly images sprang forth and surrounded it. There were men and women in smocks working with an alien technology consisting of belts and rods and braces. Parchment flew past on the belts. Those images faded and were replaced with those of other people, each poring over the text of the book.

The shard speaker moved on from the tome and the images popped out of existence.

The celestial cube drew her attention next. As the palms of her hands surrounded it, images of suns, stars and planets exploded in a visual cacophony. Arpinius started at the jumble of images, six systems apparently interspersed within one another. Stuffed into the same space, none of the systems were coherent—the cube's magnificence shattered.

The images faded. She rubbed her eyes with the heels of her hands, visibly confused by the cube.

Nyman stood as if dreaming after that. Time passed though he had no grasp of it. Strange images flickered in and out of existence, some of it familiar through his studies with Kaokesis, some reminders of temple lore or ceremony. However, the alien makeup of the images and the strange manner in which they were presented, served only to sever his connection to a reality already stretched thin by the apparent visitation from Tenedrün. The trance left him unfeeling of his own limbs, even unaware he had a corporeal body as images flickered past, his consciousness compelled down the corridors of time into scenes of the temple's long forgotten legacy.

Only when Arpinius stopped directly before him and stared at him briefly with some concern, did he once again get a glimpse of something familiar, something to reassure his soul that reality was not a fluid collage of alien beings and artifacts which seemed to present themselves willy-nilly to his benumbed mind. And yet at times, the conjured images fit into the sketchy lore of the temple as if the collage were an orderly but incomplete puzzle.

As Arpinius trolled the items around the room, Nyman's eyes followed her, anchored on the only thing he could be relatively sure pre-existed his present state of mind. She stopped before the desk and once more her hands opened up, caressing an intense hum from the air.

His eyes reluctantly left her when the desiccated skeleton suddenly sat up and formed organs, flesh, and clothing. Nyman could not tell if he was trembling or if his proximity to the hum, which seemed to reverberate inside him now, was causing his body to quake.

Nyman watched the figure shuffle through papers. It then sat for long moments eating a sandwich, seeming to savor each bite. Nyman's stomach growled and he began to salivate, the wasted corpse forgotten as the vision took him over.

The man rose and moved about the room, fingering this arti-fact and that, though they were un-aged in the archeotheurgic conjuration. His clothing changed periodically from trousers and simple shirts, to a robe, and once to some kind of full-body suit complete with a bubble for its head.

In that light, silvery suit, he passed a supine hand before the door and exited. The vision immediately switched, and the suited figure was outside, depressing the Obeisance Button. He paused several seconds at the doorway as a dark orange aura scanned across him. He reentered without mouthing the ritual phrases required of temple members.

The body suit and bubble were transformed into a breeches and tunic again as the man bent to the floor and opened a large panel big enough to admit a person. His image disappeared through the hole just as all vestiges of the conjured visions snapped out of existence.

The solidity of the cabin slammed back into Nyman's mind. He staggered, unable to balance or breathe, and stumbled backward into the wall. Arpinius ran over and placed a supporting hand beneath one arm to keep Nyman on his feet as his mind allowed reality to slowly filter back in, to take its rightful place in his disturbed psyche.

"You appear to be more sensitive than I surmised. My apologies. It can be . . . disconcerting to say the least to witness an archeotheurgic summons if one is not trained."

Arpinius let go of him as he steadied.

"What did I see?" Nyman asked, his eyes wide and glazed, still not completely focused on the firm reality of the walls and objects around him.

"Some were true visions of the past, conjured from the history of each artifact."

Nyman narrowed his eyes, unsure that such a thing was

possible though he had experienced the visions himself, and even found clarity in some of their consistencies. "Some?"

Arpinius shrugged, hesitated. "Many of the visions were . . . false, I believe," she hesitantly concluded, "the artifacts damaged, unable to provide true manifestations. I will think on it and give my report to Markom." She turned squarely toward Nyman. "You may be a good candidate to apprentice with the Prophets of the Past. Your sensitivity to the visions is a requisite condition. And rare."

Nyman sliced the air with a horizontal palm, shaking his head in bewilderment. "I already have a position here at the temple," he responded, though he was unsure what his status would be in a few days, especially after the imbroglio that this historic find had already instigated among the faithful, which would no doubt become an all-out intellectual melee after Arpinius reported her findings, whatever they may be. Throw in the apparent visitation of their god, and Nyman's future clouded so thickly he could not see where his next step might lead him.

"If the visions are false, how can this be a useful exercise?" Nyman asked. "And how can you know which are false and which true?"

Arpinius smirked and bent over to once again finger the celestial cube. "A great deal of training goes into these interpretations, acolyte," she replied, emphasizing his status. "This cube, for instance, has obviously been harmed by some non-physical manifestation. The damage, with the overlaid visions, is a sort of historical insanity that renders the object useless."

Or you don't understand what you're seeing, or how the object was used.

The acolyte's view of what he had seen differed greatly from the shard speaker's, he was sure, after listening to her vague conclusion of false visions as she might form and present them to the high priest. For him, the experience had been bewildering, but the particulars had provided some historical clarity, expanding, for instance, the possible uses of the cube.

Arpinius shrugged her narrow shoulders and turned away. She walked around the room and picked up three artifacts, plus the cone of rods. The first was the curled brown parchment. The second was a fist-sized rock of jagged-edged marble. The last was a small wooden carving. It was not intricate in detail, but very fine in finish. Shaped like a miniature obelisk, it had three small fins that steadied it in an upright stance.

Nyman was familiar with the parchment. From it, Kaokesis had interpreted the phrase, "I have brought life to this planet to stay." It was a divine handhold that had allowed the historian to maintain a firm grip on his faith, despite the dubious, and sometimes mortal, light cast on it by other findings here. However, Nyman had since studied more of the document, and he was pretty sure that the historian had mistaken the grammatical case. That in fact the possessive aspects were meant more specifically about the writer's life, rather than life on the planet in general. Nyman did not correct the error then. He was less sure about his own interpretation now, especially after meeting the presumptive god.

"We should go see High Priest Markom." The shard speaker was almost out the opening before Nyman blinked, snapping out of his reverie. He hurried out the opening to catch up, then belatedly reentered the chamber to engage in an abbreviated exit ritual—which was not uncommon among brothers in a hurry though Nyman had always tried to avoid any action that suggested anything but piety to Tenedrün—and again ducked through the opening, unsure anymore if the obeisance was even necessary.

As he ran to catch up to the prophet, he was surprised to see that the guards had changed.

"How long have we been in there?"

She stopped and turned back to him, lips pursed, eyebrows bunched once again with evident concern. "You did not feel the passage of time during the viewing?"

Nyman shrugged, confused, and gave a half-shake of his head.

"You really ought to consider a career in archeotheurgy. We have been there for nearly four hours," she finished.

Nyman stopped, stunned. A few steps later, Arpinius also halted. She turned her head, opened her mouth as if to inquire something of him, but beyond a sigh remained silent. Her stance was one of impatience to be moving forward again, one foot still placed ahead of the other, waiting to continue on.

Nyman began moving again, trodding slowly along beside her, each of the shard speaker's steps rigid with restraint. They stepped gingerly through the hole in the wall—bashed in by a fervent Brother Gerain some weeks back while on vermin duty—that led to an ancient chamber.

"I'd better get my master," he whispered, not at all sure he wanted to. He knew where his duty lay, though he was reluctant to fulfill it. Not only was there something unsettling about coming face to face with one's god, presumptive or not, but clearly Markom was looking for some ecclesiastical evidence to dispute Kaokesis's findings and was using the shard speaker to refute him. To Nyman, the celestial cube was the most powerful object in the place, whether seen in a religious context or an historical one. The fact that no one could fully understand its uses seemed reasonable, even expected. Dismissing it as damaged and useless as Arpinius was doing seemed the height of folly and ignorance to Nyman.

Arpinius nodded once in apparent acquiescence. She hesitated, then said earnestly, "A trance-like state is normal when experiencing an archeotheurgic vision. Summoning the vision is the easy part for one who has the talent, learning to maintain the necessary focus for observation and interpretation of relevant materials is much of what our school is about."

Nyman wondered how she expected to interpret the visions accurately and completely without historical relevance, and how she could so offhandedly dismiss the information gleaned from so many artifacts as false merely due to her lack of background knowledge.

He speculated silently on the possibility that he was capable of performing an archeotheurgic summons, fearful of such powerful images when all he had ever been taught to see of the past were poignant glimpses of a puzzle built by shards of artifacts, ruined buildings, bones, broken tools—enduring clues of human behavior left unwittingly behind. With the stark images of Arpinius's craft, one could weave a vibrant tapestry of the past as opposed to the few, flat puzzle pieces he now tried to place together in an unfinished collage of sparse, dim pictures—in comparison giving only a hint of the history they studied.

Arpinius continued on as Nyman, still silent, slowed to turn toward Kaokesis's apartments. She gave him a last concerned glance but said nothing.

When he reached the sparsely furnished rooms of the historian, Nyman found the old man studying some unfamiliar scrolls at his large wooden desk, a plain and unfinished workspace. Kaokesis was still draped in the loose, dusty robes he had worn to the Old Temple hours ago.

Tenedrün turned inscrutable black eyes on Nyman, his red aura returned, and peered silently at him for long moments. The acolyte froze.

"You're entering the presence of your God, boy. Don't you have something to say?"

Nyman stumbled through the lengthy obeisance Tenedrün had taught him.

"Uninspiring, to say the least, but you may enter."

Nyman stepped hesitantly into the apartments.

"So, she is finished then?"

Nyman nodded, unwilling to speak, both afraid he would be unable to convey enough meaning regarding his experience, and that he would convey too much, exposing himself as a purveyor of the charlatan's art and a nonbeliever.

"Where is she?"

The simple question allowed the acolyte voice again. "With Markom. At least, that's where she was headed when I last saw her."

"Then that is where we are headed, too."

Tenedrün paused to look at the shaken apprentice, noticing the pale skin and saucer-like eyes. "What's wrong, boy? Haven't you gotten used to me popping in for a visit yet?"

"Master, I . . . that is, uh, Tenedrün, I . . . the summons, the archeotheurgic summons?"

"Yes, I'm familiar with their terminology."

"I saw the visions she conjured," he admitted, eyes downcast. His shame came not from the visions, however, but from the decision he knew he had made regarding his relationship with the historian. Though Tenedrün's presence may render his decision moot.

He did not know when he would have to do it, nor how it would come about, but he knew, instinctively, that self-preservation would force him to abandon his master when the time came. And the time would come. All indications were such that Markom would reject the historian's conclusions, else why bring in the shard speaker? Nyman sensed, as did Markom, that the temple historian's conclusions would invalidate some long-held rituals and lore. And that assumed that Kaokesis remained himself. If he assumed the personage of their god, well, there was no telling what kind of ecclesiastical conflagration that might cause.

Too much change too fast was not good for temple faith. And Nyman knew, just like Kaokesis knew, that such things must change slowly, if at all, else all core beliefs come into question.

What role the god might play in this, he had no clue.

Tenedrün paused, squinting under brows bunched with concern for the boy. "Apparently you are convinced the summons was no parlor trick, nor anything she conjured simply for your viewing."

Nyman shook his head, his eyes still tracing the lines between inlaid tiles on the floor. "I do not think so, Tenedrün," he whispered.

"And what do you think of me? Am I a parlor trick? Some false presentation of your imagination? What of your sanity, boy, do you believe it still intact?"

Nyman did not try to convey all that had gone through his head. He did not address specifically his worry about Kaokesis, nor about the falsehood of the temple faith, nor about the upheaval that could come of the Old Temple discovery or the god's presence, much less both. He did not say he feared less for his own sanity, that his personal clarity would probably not suffer even if the temple's faith was shattered. He only nodded once, afraid still to speak.

"Tell me about the visions on the way to the high priest's office," he ordered, slapping the boy on the back to get him moving.

It should have been a ten-minute walk. But once Nyman began to explain what he remembered of Arpinius's summons,

Tenedrün kept stopping to delve deeper into the visions of forgotten human behavior that the shard speaker had seemingly caressed from the durable legacies they had found in the room.

Nearly an hour later, they finally arrived at Markom's office. Before entering the outer chamber, Nyman glanced nervously at his Lord and master. The god smiled back and gestured to the acolyte to enter. Nyman nearly puked as he gripped the handle and pulled, blood and bile seemingly in a race through his chest toward his head.

The two were admitted into the plush confines of the high priest's inner office, where they found Arpinius conferring with Markom. Nyman stole a last glance at Tenedrün, and saw that the red aura had disappeared.

"Come, come in," Markom waved them to his desk, smiling. He ushered them toward a couple of cushioned chairs that sat opposite his own at the desk. Arpinius sat off to one side, as close to the historian as to Markom.

When they were seated, Markom said to Nyman, "I hear you've had quite the experience." His tone was jovial, yet his eyes were narrowed, piercing. "Arpinius said she was surprised at how sensitive you were during her summonings."

Nyman shrugged and looked to his toes sticking out the end of worn sandals. He remained silent, desperate to bide his time before committing to anything aloud, his thoughts already careening away from accepted canon. The acolyte twitched a nervous glance toward his mentor.

Kaokesis motioned to the artifacts that Arpinius had removed from the chamber sitting on the high priest's desk. He began to finger them and growled, "Why are these here?"

Nyman released his breath, relieved the focus had been removed from him, yet unsure if Kaokesis really did not know, despite their conversation on the way here, or if he was just playing dumb.

"Arpinius deemed them the most important artifacts in the room," Markom explained.

The historian raised a quizzical brow. "Really?"

"The other artifacts are quite mad," she explained.

"Mad? Mad? How can an inanimate object be mad? It has no psyche, no mind, no emotions with which to go mad from," he demanded, aghast at her conclusion. "It is more likely that you did not understand what you conjured from the other items."

"Each artifact is the product of all the qualities you name possessed by humans, and more. Such effects are passed on by handlers, by surroundings. Unfortunately, sometimes trauma can jumble the images so that they become nonsense, confused," she asserted, as if explaining to a first year student the nuances of an archeotheurgic summons.

"I think it more likely that you are unable to place those images in your ignorant little universe because you have nothing with which to reference them. You have not studied any of the material that existed before this find, nor cross-checked any items with the room for consistent knowledge. I daresay our cafeteria would seem mad to you shortly after lunch time!"

"As it does to me," Markom calmly interjected.

Arpinius shrugged, unaffected by the diatribe.

"Now, now, Kaokesis, our esteemed prophet did find some things consistent with your claims. For instance, she was able to ascertain, as you did, that our god's real name is in fact Tenedrün. I can only imagine that through faulty record keeping or shorthand it was attenuated over the centuries. And I think you'll be happy to know that I've already sent out a directive to correct this problem," Markom beamed.

Kaokesis frowned, unappeased. "That is a question of miniscule importance," he growled. "Irrelevant to the more important questions of the origin of the god and his myths. An origin whose visions Arpinius and Nyman have seen and, as I stated," he wagged a finger as if correcting a child, "have served only to confuse her; and in turn the council and your esteemed self, High Priest."

For the first time, Markom frowned. Nyman did not like the frown. It seemed to signal some change in attitude, an inner conclusion Markom had come to as to the fate of Kaokesis, and hence himself.

"Then it is too late for the council, Kaokesis, because they have been informed of the findings. And," he said, holding up a hand to forestall the historian's aborted objections. "I am in the process of forming an official stance on those findings. In fact, well on my way." He indicated a parchment on his desk marked with unfinished text.

Kaokesis turned a calculated stare at the high priest and his archeotheurgist, then went on more calmly than Nyman would have believed possible.

"What is so sane about these three artifacts?"

Markom motioned for Arpinius to answer.

"The marble shard is in fact from a local quarry lost in the same earthquake which temple lore states has destroyed and buried the Old Temple. I have been able to give pointed coordinates to where it is buried so that your church may use the substance again to build. Markom has indicated to me that such was used on much of the Old Temple, though those structures and most early histories were destroyed or buried in the devastation some two-hundred-and-twenty years ago."

"A find of some possible significance, though again not relevant to church doctrine."

Arpinius waited until all was silent for several seconds

before continuing on. "The parchment and ink are also of local origin, though the language is one unfamiliar to any—as you have no doubt already discovered."

"Also of possible note," he conceded, "when we can fully translate it."

"Don't you see, Kaokesis, it is obviously the hand of Ten, er, Tenedrün. A major religious artifact! It may be years before we understand what is in it, but what a wealth of ecclesiastical lore it must contain!"

Despite the high priest's excitement, Kaokesis only shrugged.

"Maybe. Although I think 'years' may be an overstatement. There are other documents in the same language scattered throughout the room," he informed them, as if they had been missing the obvious.

"Uh, well, yes, we'll chat about that later," Markom replied, suddenly not as enthusiastic.

"And the last?" Koakesis inquired of Arpinius.

"It is a carving made by whom your church has always referred to as Rector Primus, the first of your order. It is clearly a replica of some obelisk, and just as clearly its memories have shown it was made as worship to Tenedrün."

"You've got an entire room down there, preserved in time, and that is all you can conclude?" Kaokesis chided. "Well, eliminating everything you cannot immediately make sense of must do wonders for your clarity. However, our faith cannot suffer pointed ignorance. Your dismissal of our past threatens to turn the rituals of sanctity and piety into vague gestures of simple-minded obeisance!"

"That is almost correct, Historian," the high priest answered. "But it is not Arpinius who is at fault." Markom sounded suddenly proper, playing to full his role as High Priest and Father Divulger. "What you need to understand is that any manifestation of faith constructed by imperfect beings set up as worship to the perfect God Tenedrün, is itself bound to be imperfect."

Nyman saw Kaokesis's end as temple historian plainly now, and dreaded what might become of him. Kaokesis looked at the room and saw mysteries just beginning to be unraveled, a beacon of ecclesiastical light ready to help show them the proper path. Markom, it seemed, saw the mysteries as solved, identified for belief and properly placed in the temple lore.

The old historian merely squinted and remained silent, thus managing to maintain his standing for a little while longer.

Markom smiled. "Come now, I have a surprise for you. A peace offering if you will."

Kaokesis remained silent, as the high priest went on, somewhat less enthusiastically after getting no response to his attempt at placating the historian. "When this chamber was discovered, I wondered in what complex in the Old Temple it could have resided. I had certainly never heard of anything of its likeness. So I decided to excavate toward it from the north as well. I have just gotten word that the excavation has turned up something relevant to this whole discussion. Something fantastic, in fact, if the messages are to be believed!"

Kaokesis maintained a stoic silence. Markom frowned.

"I was hoping you would accompany us down to the site, Kaokesis."

"And watch as this charlatan dismisses it as mad?"

"Do not let your feelings toward the prophet affect your zeal for your faith, Brother," Markom chided. "Besides, I am not convinced such a summons will be necessary in this case."

Kaokesis acquiesced with a shrug and turned to Nyman. "I left some notes down in the Old Temple chamber. Please fetch them for me."

Nyman, only too glad to be released from the pressure of this meeting, leapt to his feet.

"Um." Markom stopped him with one finger held up. Everyone froze, eyes on the high priest. He lowered his hand. "Yes, well, please hurry. Meet us outside the north gate of the compound. From there you can see all of the activity surrounding the excavation."

Nyman hurried out of the office and took a breath of relief once he reached the hallway. He tried to clear his mind of worry, of the choices he might have to make or that may be made for him. His philosophical flexibility had allowed him entrance into the temple, and he hoped it would carry him through this crisis. Kaokesis, however, was not flexible on matters of doctrine, nor history—and the two were waging a war for Nyman's soul. The acolyte was afraid it would rip asunder his standing in the church. Nyman wondered what Markom's excavation might have uncovered. He was not hopeful that it would aid Kaokesis.

After leaving the temple proper, the eastern grounds came into view as Nyman mindlessly drifted that way. He had started taking this route several years ago because it was the least populated part of the massive compound, its sanctuary being the oldest, its amenities being the most crude. He had continued to use it because of his infatuation with the cook's daughter who was hired to clean and maintain the sanctuary proper.

He emerged on the south side of the old sanctuary onto the open mezzanine, which overlooked the courtyard below. As he passed by the double doors leading in, his hand brushed gently across the brass handles adorning the massive wooden portals. He paused for a moment, licked his lips in worry at being late to the excavation, and entered the chamber anyway.

With his head half-bowed, his hands folded before him, he

wandered sedately to a balcony seat overlooking the main sanctuary chamber below. The ornate woodwork of pews, windows, dais, and rails disappeared from his mind as he put on devout airs as an excuse to kneel and clandestinely watch the girl below.

Despite the loose clothing and billowy smock she wore, her grace was evident to him this time as every time. His worries disappeared for a few moments as his sight savored every subtle movement she made. Despite the longing he felt for her, he had never approached her. Such a tryst would have gone against temple code, of course, though many brothers committed that violation or worse. He just did not want to jeopardize his standing and his studies.

He loved his studies. He spoke three languages before entering the temple, and had doubled that since arriving. Unfortunately, whereas he could read and recite the approved histories of God and Temple, he had yet to figure out how to communicate to the eldest daughter of the head cook his simplest desires.

Nyman rose and hurried out of the sanctuary balcony feeling ill, as usual. Once on the mezzanine, he leaned over the stone railing and took several deep breaths to regain his composure.

Below, he saw Brother Gerain. With his holy rat in a gilded cage, he gesticulated fervently to the dozen or so brothers looking on. Nyman could not make out the words, but suddenly Gerain set the cage on a bench and the crowd kneeled before it.

The acolyte chuckled and shook his head at the thought of what Markom's reaction might be if he witnessed the proceedings below.

Recovered, Nyman continued on his way. He trotted down the steps from the mezzanine and continued eastward toward the ruins of the Old Temple. Once there, he slipped inside and quickly made his way downward toward the metal room to fetch Kaokesis's notes.

As he approached the bottom landing of the crumbling stone steps, he heard indistinct voices echoing up through the dilapidated corridor. Slowly, he snuck the rest of the way down.

He peered cautiously around the corner and saw some rough-clothed workmen, spattered with a gray substance, chatting with two guards. *What were they working on?*

Nyman turned the opposite way, toward the room of metal walls, and was surprised to find that the wall originally knocked into by Brother Gerain had been squared off and cleaned up. He wondered if they were going to finish the entry-way, make it more accessible.

However, once he reached the room, he saw that it too had been cleaned up, but was also half-sealed. Stone and mortar stood thigh-high in the opening!

The acolyte looked around, nearly in a panic. What should he do? Obviously Markom had decided this room had caused enough problems and was going to seal it off, and the artifacts with it. Without them, Kaokesis's conclusions would be rendered worse than moot, possibly even heretical. That did not bode well for the historian.

Nyman stepped over the unfinished wall and looked for the notes Kaokesis had requested. He didn't see them anywhere. It would seem odd that he had left anything of his studies down here in any case. Kaokesis always made sure his notes remained with him, or in his apartments where he could get to them any time, day or night.

Nyman shrugged and took one last scan of the room. His eyes passed over the celestial cube. The acolyte licked his dry lips, then snuck to the doorway to peer down the ancient corridor. Still no one came. With one sweaty palm, he snatched the cube and buried it deep in a robe pocket.

He scooted out the opening, whacking his head painfully and stumbling into the pile of debris created by the workmen. Rubbing his painful scalp to make sure there was no blood, he bolted up the corridor and emerged through the squared-off opening.

As he started toward the stairs, the voices drew closer. Nyman froze, then turned around and began walking back toward the opening.

He heard a deep baritone voice order, "Hold it right there, Brother."

Nyman, a look as close to innocent on his face as he could muster, turned.

"Yes?" he inquired of the two guardsmen who accompanied four workmen.

"Markom has declared that area strictly off limits. Nobody is to go in there."

"But," Nyman protested weakly.

"No exceptions," one of the guards interrupted.

Nyman forced out a sigh. "We shall see about that." He strode past the six men and up the stairs, his heart hammering at his chest, his belly aquiver.

He hurried to the north gate and then down toward the excavation. The workmen, seemingly told to expect him, directed him beneath the rubble and past large stones into an artificial cavern. Unconsciously fingering the cube in his pocket, Nyman followed the tunnel some hundred paces in before sighting Markom and Kaokesis. As the acolyte approached them, he snatched his hand from his pocket. He looked up guiltily, but that was quashed by what he saw behind the two men.

Lying lengthwise on the ground, its silverish body

battered, broken, and rusted, was the full-size version of the miniature obelisk, which Markom now nervously fingered. The huge chamber was only partially lit by torches and lamps as workmen set about the task of clearing some space around the fallen monument.

"The room of metal walls is inside that?" Nyman whispered.

Markom frowned, then looked briefly at the wooden miniature version in his hand before quickly pocketing it.

Kaokesis's black eyes gleamed. "Did you get my notes, boy?"

Nyman shook his head, and moved closer. Kaokesis was not himself. The acolyte restrained the urge to piss himself.

"He was not able to," Markom declared, turning his back on the presumptive god, unaware of the transformation that had taken place once again in the historian.

The high priest shouted to his workmen. "Never mind that," he ordered. "Everyone clear out." The workmen shrugged, mumbling to each other, but content to do as directed.

"What do you mean, he wasn't able to?" Tenedrün finally asked, as the last workman filed out. Markom stood with his back to the two, staring at the supine obelisk.

"I have decided to seal off the chamber. The guards were told that under no circumstances was anyone to be granted access while this was going on. The same shall be done here."

Neither Tenedrün nor Nyman spoke.

As if in answer to an unasked question, Markom continued softly, almost to himself. "There are no answers for us here." He stared long at the obelisk, his hand straying to its miniature in his robe pocket.

Nyman stood face to face with his god, filled with the

clarity of his situation, doubts as to the answers swirling through his mind.

Tenedrün whispered, "Leave us, boy. Leave the complex and head north, now. Go to the first hill you see and climb it. Dismiss the workers. Tell them to return tomorrow for further instructions."

Nyman began to slowly back away. Markom removed the wooden miniature from his pocket and tossed it on a nearby pile of rubble. Tenedrün's aura dissipated as the high priest turned back.

"Is there no room in your faith, Father, for such remarkable artifacts as these?" Nyman heard Kaokesis say. He turned and picked up his pace, suddenly eager to be away.

"Faith is not a concrete thing, Brother. One does not come face-to-face with one's god, or even the artifacts of that god's origin, at least not in such tangible manifestation as this, and expect to maintain the simple integrity of belief," he answered, his words now echoing.

Nyman ceased eavesdropping then, the pounding of his heart drowning out the now distant words. Once he reached the sunlight of the excavation site outside, he dispatched the orders as given to him by Tenedrün, and made his reluctant way across a nearby cornfield, through even rows, and up the terraces of the nearest hill.

Once he reached the fourth terrace, he felt a rumble beneath his feet. The ground jumped, sending him sprawling across the dirt. The ground continued to lurch as he struggled toward the crest. Once he reached the top, it was all he could do to keep on his feet.

Nyman turned back to observe the temple complex. It seemed to be at the center of the quake. A number of buildings had begun to collapse above the violently shifting ground. People were streaming out of the complex like crazed animals from their burrow, the lines of them jumped and heaved, broke and reformed.

The walls surrounding the complex collapsed, the excavation of the Old Temple almost indistinguishable from the ruin of the new temple. When the quake finally ceased, the silence was broken by the wail of injured, the cry of the dispossessed, the anguish of those cast out by god and temple.

Nyman saw Brother Gerain picking his way through the rubble, trying to escape the temple's holocaust. He held the cage with his holy rat in one hand, and the hand of the washerwoman's daughter in the other. They escaped to the west, a handful of followers in their wake.

Nyman watched the aftermath in fascination, all the time fingering the cobalt cube in his pocket. What chance he had of translating the spoken language, manifested by the cube when activated, had possibly died in the crush of falling stones during the temple's collapse. Nevertheless, he pressed one of the sides and began to listen, mesmerized by the mysteries it held.

GREGORY J. GLANZ

Greg is a homebrewer and biking enthusiast. Surprisingly, they go exceedingly well together as more and more microbrews chase bicyclists across the trails. In his spare time, of which there is plenty right now, he is an IT consultant in central Iowa.

facebook.com/gglanz

twitter.com/gjg_write

LIGHT KEEPER (ᎠᏦᏍᎦ ᎤᎦᏎᏗ)

A'LIYA SPINNER

Trigger Warning: Mention of recently deceased relative

G ravel crunched beneath the tires of the Saturn as it rolled into a poorly marked spot at the end of the meandering, unpaved road. A tilting signpost just ahead, bathed in the glow of headlights, announced "VISITOR PARKING" in aggressive capitals, as if hoping to be seen past the long drive that preceded the small lot. Beyond, less assertive and less well-lit, was a wooden sign that read "Whitefish Point State Park." The stakes anchoring it to the ground were hidden by bunches of switchgrass, and the paint lining the words was flaking from age.

It was unlikely these trails were frequented by any local groundskeeping services; the underbrush had overgrown what little of the path the driver could see in the headlight-diffused gloom of the stormy night. It wasn't where he had been hoping to end up, but it was where he had come by necessity; the road was becoming slick with the icy rain of November, and it was only going to get more treacherous as the night deepened. He didn't trust himself—or the twenty-one-year-old stick shift— to complete the last leg of their journey to a motel. It was only by luck that the first exit he'd found had brought him close to the place he'd been looking for all along: *Whitefish Point,* a small peninsula of land jutting into the mighty Lake Superior. He hadn't known about the State Park, which, judging by the looks of it, wasn't surprising; it must've been decommissioned and abandoned years ago.

Matthew Kidwell shifted the car into neutral and let out the clutch, not yet decided on his next step. Vibrations from the rumbling engine passed through his seat as the Saturn idled, shivering in the rain. Its wipers slid noisily across the windshield every thirty seconds or so, giving him a few moments of visibility before thick streams of rain pooled on the glass. Thunder rolled in the distance, past the shadowy tops of pine trees. The storm was worsening; there was no returning to the main road tonight. Matthew took the keys out of the ignition and pulled the parking break into a secure position. Pounding rain on the roof replaced the growling of the engine.

The sensible thing would be to lean his seat back and try to sleep. Or, perhaps even better, use his cellphone to call for a tow truck to take him to the nearest town. But neither option crossed his mind for longer than a moment. The satchel draped across the passenger's seat wordlessly beckoned to him. No matter how firmly he gripped the wheel or how squarely he stared ahead at the dark woods, he knew he was going to give in.

"*Damnit*," he murmured under his breath, knowing what he had to do. Waiting for the storm to pass before backtracking to the more popular beaches at Tahquamenon Falls State Park would mean at least another day in Michigan. He had developed a hatred for this wet, cold, and *miserable* state during his three day pilgrimage through the Lower Peninsula to the tip of the Upper. The sooner he got home to Oklahoma, to his fiancé and work, the happier he would be.

There was something sadistically poetic about stumbling through a forest in the darkness and rain, anyways—penance for the way Matthew had treated the man whose last request he was now committed to carrying out. The old Tsalagi *had* specified that it was "better if it was raining," though why the weather mattered to an old heirloom or an even older lake was lost to Matthew.

"If I trip and break my neck in those woods, Grandpa," he muttered, "we're going to exchange some *coarse* words in Heaven." He shoved his phone into the pocket of his jeans, grabbed the satchel from the seat beside him and a flashlight from the dash, threw open the door, and stepped out into the rain. The Saturn locked with a satisfying, mechanical *click* before the keys, too, found their way into his pockets.

It wasn't as cold as he was expecting. A local he'd met at a gas station had commented with sincere wonder at the "mildness" of this year's winter, but Matthew hadn't really been expecting a November night in Michigan to be anything less than hellishly frigid. Now it seemed he was wrong. Though he wasn't particularly comfortable as he stood in the rain in nothing but a light jacket, he didn't think his extremities were in danger of freezing off.

Matthew switched on the flashlight. It was a weighty tool, and its broad cone of light speared through the rain and night. Swinging the satchel over his shoulder—it was not heavy, for it had but one item within—and wrapping his jacket tighter around himself to prevent the total soaking of his shirt, he started away from the parking lot and toward the trees.

The sign denoting the entrance to Whitefish Point looked to be in even worse condition than the one at the entrance to the park. Not only was it listing back and to the side, but weeds were growing out of the wood itself, from deep fissures of rot that had chipped away at the edges. It'd definitely been at least a year, probably longer, since park rangers had been here. He wondered why. The gravel road preceding it had been long and winding, but not completely inaccessible, and he didn't see any warning signs hastily erected nearby to declare these trails closed to trespassers. Even stripped of its mantle of State Park, surely such a scenic and wooded spot would be popular among teenagers and adventurers—at least enough to justify local upkeep. Quite unusually, it looked to Matthew that this far end of Whitefish Point had just been abandoned. Maybe there was something the locals knew that he didn't.

It was a silly thought. Michigan may have been unpleasant, but it wasn't lawless. If there were a bear den or some other hazard nearby, the state department would have made at least a minimal effort to keep visitors out. He determined the path was safe, just not well-tended.

Matthew clenched his jaw and wiped rain from his eyes as he started down the overgrown trail. Twigs snapped beneath his feet, announcing his arrival to hidden woodland creatures as he plunged into the shrouded forest. It did not take long for the dense trees to swallow him, cutting him off from all signs of modern civilization.

Were he not already well-acquainted with hiking, Matthew suspected he may have easily gotten lost along the winding trail. The main path, distinguished by the occasional weathered marker and the remnants of mulch or plank walkways, was often intersected by trampled underbrush left by processions of deer in search of grazing ground. Anyone less familiar with woodlands would likely have strayed in the darkness and the rain, but Matthew had spent enough adolescent weekends hunting with his grandfather to recognize the faint impression of hoof prints in the mud, criss-crossing the true trail and wandering off into the forest.

But even armed with a flashlight and a lifetime of experience, Matthew was forced to go slowly and carefully. He aimed the light downwards, scanning for hazardous roots or burrows, and then up at the woods, searching for a way forward. Occasionally, his light passed over a rustling patch of bracken or a trembling, low-hanging tree branch from which some startled animal had rapidly departed. He flinched every time, expecting the disturbed creature to lunge out at him in anger. None ever did.

"You're slipping, Kidwell," he grumbled to himself as he worked his way down a treacherously severe slope, feeling the mud shift beneath his feet and threaten his balance. He nearly fell several times, saved only by grabbing nearby branches and spewing expletives.

Growing up near the Cherokee Nation reservation in Oklahoma, Matthew had once been much more comfortable in the darkness and rain, camping with his sister and cousins under the stars in all sorts of weather. There had been no trails in *those* days—only endless, forested mountains—and yet he had never lost his way nor his footing. His great-grandfather, the eccentric founder of the company that had brought the Kidwell's their fortune, referred to it as their family "gift," so long as they did not stray too far from the reservation and their people, they would always know their way home.

But the "gift," as he had called it, died with him. Several weeks after his great-grandfather's funeral, Matthew and his sister had gotten lost in the Ouachitas for two days before local authorities had finally found them, freezing and starving. That event had permanently stifled his attraction to the wilderness, and it wasn't until he'd met his adventure-hungry fiancé that he'd dared to venture back into the mountains, rekindling an appreciation for the untamed forest.

Something about the Michigan woods stirred deep memories of the Ouachitas in Matthew. He wasn't lost here. In fact, as the path continued to slope downwards toward the shoreline, the trail was becoming easier to follow. But there was a feeling of *unease*. His skin prickled, not from the cold, but from the sensation of eyes among the shaking trees. There was none of the comfort of hiking the mountains of Oklahoma, Arkansas, and Kentucky, where Tsalagi blood ran deep and old. Yet, it was to *Michigan* that his grandfather had, two weeks ago, asked Matthew to take the heirloom burdening his satchel. He had even specified the Northernmost point of Michigan, to the shores of Lake Superior, the mightiest of the five Great Lakes. It was the memory of this request that kept Matthew from turning back, even as the eerie feeling of being watched crescendoed. Thunder rolled overhead, drowning out the rattling of the trees as the wind whipped their branches together.

When the bellowing of the storm abated and the normal din of heavy rain and rustling trees resumed, Matthew became aware, at last, of a third sound: *waves*. Ahead of him, not yet visible through the trees, he heard waves crashing against a nearby shore. He was close. His pace quickened, less wary of obstacles on the ground as he aimed his light outwards, hoping to catch a glimpse of reflections from the surface of the lake through the dark pillars of the forest.

Lightning flashed across the sky, washing the forest around him in pigmentless shades of grey. Something moved overhead at the same moment, but Matthew caught only its shadow piercing the rain before the light subsided and shrouded the figure again. A crack of thunder followed, timed perfectly to the way a branch overhanging the trail ahead sagged.

Waves of powerful and illogical fear coursed through him; his free hand made the Sign of the Cross, more out of habit than faith. It lasted for just a moment, causing his muscles to tense and his heart to race; then his panic was gone as quickly and inexplicably as it had arrived. By the time the thunder faded away, Matthew had regained control of himself. He raised the flashlight and fixed the lurking shadow in its beam.

A bird perched serenely before him. Its flat, pale face and round eyes were unmistakably those of a barn owl, a common breed that roosted in many of the old buildings around the reservation. Framed in Matthew's light, the bird glanced to the side and shifted its mottled wings. Its wicked talons squeezed tighter around the bowing branch.

"You scared the hell out of me," Matthew scolded, feeling a little foolish for how he reacted. He should've known it would be a nocturnal bird and nothing more, although it was strange that this one had chosen to hunt in such atrocious weather. In response to his admonishing, the bird twisted its neck to look at him straight-on. Immediately, the tingly, uneasy feeling of eyes returned, crawling down his spine.

"Have you been *following* me?" he accused.

His silent counsel remained so, the wind stirring its feathers. Matthew had never heard of owls taking interest in people like coyotes or crows did while scrounging for scraps, but this one certainly seemed to be regarding him with a certain level of expectation. *Why?*

A memory surfaced from the murky depths of his childhood—a story told to him by his grandfather, back when the man had been lucid enough to impart on his grandchildren the Tsalagi superstitions of *his* father, the great-grandfather whose alleged mistake Matthew was now tasked to correct. Matthew's mother, a staunch Irish Catholic, had discouraged Tsalagi traditions in her household, and his father, who was both mild-mannered and Cornell-educated, had not protested; he'd never put much stock in the stories of his people, and intended to raise his children in a "modern household." But Matthew and his sister had always listened with the insatiable curiosity of youth to the myths their grandfather spun for them, the ghost of which he was trying to recall.

Be wary of the owl, his grandfather's raspy voice whispered in Matthew's ear, but the rest of the memory was too indistinct to hear. The relationship between Tsalagi and owls was something important—*that* he remembered, and nothing else. He cursed himself for not listening better to the stories of his people. The owl watched him with expressionless passivity, unbothered by the harsh glow of his flashlight.

"Come on, Kidwell, it's just a bird." Matthew closed his eyes and drew in a deep, calming breath, deciding it didn't matter what his grandfather had said. There must've been something strange in the Michigan air to make him think that an *owl* might be a marker of the supernatural. He had inherited his father's flavorless pragmatism; even being raised in the Church could not shake his personal apathy for spiritualism, though he loved the joy he saw on his sister's face during the homilies. Christ had helped her through their family's adversities, just as the spirit guides that their grandfather claimed to see had comforted him all the way to the bitter end. Matthew's faith had always been in more tangible powers, and so he had coped with the crushing weight of his grandfather's sickness and company misfortune by working himself nearly to the death.

But now, with his fiancé, new job, and soon-to-be-born nephew, Matthew had the chance to start down a brighter path. All that lingered of his "bad years" was his grandfather's last request, and tonight, that, too, would be finished.

A flash of lightning illuminated the inside of Matthew's eyelids, and he blinked open his eyes. The owl was gone. The branch it had perched on swayed in the winds of the storms, unburdened. He hadn't heard it take flight; he wasn't sure how long he'd been standing there with his eyes squeezed shut as he steeled himself against thoughts of his family.

Readjusting his flashlight to aim past where the owl had formerly barred his way, Matthew caught a glimpse of the tell-tale glimmer of water. The "itch" of being watched had departed with the bird, and he felt no more eyes from the forest. *It's almost over*, he thought. *Then I can go home. And I am never coming back to Michigan.* This he promised most vehemently.

The shoreline was becoming increasingly visible as the trail sloped gently downwards to meet it. Through the rain that pounded his back and the wind that grabbed at his jacket,

Matthew saw the outlines of waves, roused by the storm. The water thrashed, churning and roaring, and each crash of the rearing, foaming crests mingled with the rumble of the thunder overhead to create a cacophony that Matthew cautiously approached.

The trees around him began to thin as the mud beneath his shoes became grainy and more sand-like. The storm winds were stronger here, without the protection of the forest. In the distance, lightning touched down somewhere on the multitude of small islands dotting the shallows around the shore; for a moment, the whole world seemed to be illuminated in glittering silver, washing over the tumultuous waves and making them shine with reflected light. Then the water was shrouded in darkness once again, and the night hemmed in around him. Somehow his flashlight felt both defiantly powerful and woefully inadequate at the same time.

It was not the most impressive shoreline. If this was the ultimate destination of the trails, Matthew could see why they had been abandoned in favor of more scenic patches of beach a few miles up the road. The disturbed waves rammed against the rocky shore, which was hazardously uneven underfoot. He carefully worked his way to the edge of the water, his shoes sliding on wobbly stones, slick with moss and rain. He silently thanked his years of mountain climbing and good Tsalagi genes for giving him the ability to balance on such unsteady ground after a few near-falls that would've bruised his tailbone and soaked his clothes.

At last, he reached the edge of the lake, the water lapping at his shoes. The winds were whipping the lake into an angry frenzy farther out, beyond the island buffers that spared the shore from the worst of the storm, and tugged insistently at his jacket as if trying to pull him into the shallows. Matthew had heard many stories about this lake—which his grandfather had called *Gichi-gami*—and its tendency to swallow ships in its icy depths. Memories of those legends percolated into his mind as he gazed out over the water and imagined how his ancestors must have trembled at the sight.

"Okay," he muttered under his breath, using his free hand to fish inside the satchel for its sole occupant. "Let's get this over with." His fingers closed around something cool to the touch, angular, and about the size of a baseball: the burden that his grandfather had left to him. He pulled it from the bag and held it out for the wind and rain to taste.

Lightning flashed and reflected from the gemstone's pristine surface. It was opalescent pale and roughly spherical—a family heirloom that had once sat on his great-grandfather's desk before being passed down to his grandfather, who kept it hidden away and wrapped in deerskin. Now it was Matthew's; *he* had wanted to sell the strange gem, hoping it was exotic enough to cover some of the mounting expense of his upcoming wedding, but his grandfather's dying wish had been explicitly clear—*cast the Ulun'suti into Lake Superior.*

Even if he did not prescribe to the superstitions of his people—especially around spirits and unfinished business—Matthew respected his grandfather enough to honor this last request. Tonight, the "Ulun'suti" would be laid to rest forever in Superior's depths, and Matthew could return to his life in peaceful, landlocked Oklahoma.

There was another flash of lightning, quickly followed by a tremendous crack of thunder. This time the reflected flash did not fade when the heavens fell dark; a soft, white glow remained inside of the angular gem, faint, but growing in intensity. Matthew blinked and switched off his flashlight, plunging the shore into thick darkness—darkness that was partially alleviated by the light of the Ulun'suti in his palm.

"*What the hell . . .*" he whispered under his breath, holding the heirloom closer to his face, turning it over, looking for a mechanism or any sign of tampering with its natural surface, even shining the flashlight through it, looking for imperfections. He was no trained or talented jeweler, but figured he *should* have been able to tell if there was a light bulb or miniature solar panel inside of his family's oldest treasure; he saw nothing. The gem seemed to glow of its own volition, brightening even as he inspected it.

Matthew had googled *Ulun'suti* the day after his grandfather had tasked him with its disposal. The name derived from an old Tsalagi myth, and referred to a luminous, magical gemstone that could be collected from the forehead of spirit-serpents called Uktena, should a Tsalagi warrior be brave enough to slay one. The Ulun'suti granted its owner good fortune and powerful medicine, but if the warrior were to die before laying the stone to rest, its power would haunt him and his family as punishment for tormenting the powerful spirit from which it came. The story, however ridiculous, was what had driven Matthew so far to fulfill his grandfather's request; their family's misfortunate had worsened with the old Tsalagi's sickness. His grandfather must've placed the blame on great-grandfather's old paperweight. If it had glowed like this in the past, he easily understood how his more superstitious family members came to attribute their bad luck to supernatural causes, with an appropriately supernatural scapegoat.

"What are you?" Matthew asked the mysterious stone. It was shining so brightly in his palm he didn't even need his flashlight. Had he not already come so far, he would've had the heirloom appraised to find out what mechanism or property was creating such a powerful light. But he was already on the shores of its final destiny, and ultimately content to let its light remain a mystery.

"Speak now or forever keep your peace." He waited for a

beat, expecting and receiving nothing but the low grumble of thunder and crashing waves in response. There was no magic in this rock; it was merely a curiosity that had stoked the imaginations of several generations of curious Kidwells. Matthew rolled his shoulder and pulled back his arm, preparing to toss the jewel as far out into the heaving waters as he was able.

Something moved in the lake, out by the islands but rapidly growing closer, making him pause and lower his hand. The water rippled and splashed *against* the wind-thrashed waves of the storm; he tracked the disturbance by a faint light, roaming just beneath the surface, fading and strengthening as it bobbed up and down. He thought it might be a buoy yanked free of its anchor by the storm, but it was far too large, and far too . . . long.

The roving light grew closer to shore. Matthew took a nervous step backwards, flailing for balance as he slipped on a lichen-covered stone. The jewel in his palm was almost blindingly bright now, blotting out the world around him.

The lake erupted. Water sprayed in every direction, drenching the few parts of Matthew not already soaked by the storm. He flinched, throwing up his arms to shield his face; through the stone's haze of light and his splayed fingers, he saw a shadow surging out of the depths, maybe two dozen meters from shore. Its form was indistinct in the darkness of the night, but he saw at its peak a fierce beacon, just like the one he held in his hand. He squinted, trying to make out the tall, shifting shadow; it looked something like a lighthouse as it towered above him, but the rain diffused its glow, and he could not quite distinguish its features. Forked lightning touched down on a distant island, illuminating the night.

Not a lighthouse.

Matthew tried to run; his feet slipped on the rain-slicked shore and he fell, crying out in pain as sharp-edged rocks dug into his thighs and back, nearly knocking the wind out of him. The flashlight was jostled from his hand; he felt it spin away in the darkness and watched its beam tumble and flicker until it toppled to the ground, pointed toward the undulating base of the towering, scaled . . .

"*Hi Tsalagis?*"

Matthew flinched as the sounds rolled over him like thunder, deep and guttural. He wanted to release the Ulun'suti, to cover his ears and eyes until the nightmarish vision ended, but his grip refused to relax. His other hand was moving on its own accord, too, scrabbling against the slick rocks as he tried to push himself up.

"*Hi Tsalagis?*"

He braced himself. The noise vibrated him to his bones as it passed overhead, rustling the leaves of the storm-whipped branches and shaking the rain that fell from the sky. He clenched his teeth at the sensation, even as he realized it was not just meaningless sound, but *words*. The first syllable—*hee*—he did not know, but the rest he thought he recognized.

"Tsa—Tsalagi?" He stammered, calling to the light as it swayed above him. "My name is Matthew Kidwell; I'm Tsalagi. Well—I'm—I'm half . . ."

"*Tsalagis hiwonsigi?*" The atonal bellow crashed over his words and swept them away. Matthew felt like the air itself was being forced out of his lungs by some unseen force. He struggled to breathe; the wind was too fast and angry to be inhaled. Rain pelted his face, running in rivulets down his brow and into his eyes, blurring his vision alongside undignified, terrified tears.

When he did not reply, the phrase repeated, booming over the lake: *Tsalagis hiwonsigi?* He did not know what it meant. He did not speak the language of his people, despite his grandfather's insistence that he must. Even the sounds were strange to him.

"Please," he begged, not knowing what he was asking for. "I can't understand what you're saying." He could not muster the energy to raise his voice to anything stronger than a whisper.

The light moved. It began to lower, coming closer to Matthew. The Ulun'suti in his hand seemed to throb in response, as if the two were connected. At last, he found his footing and rose shakily to his feet, clutching the glowing stone in front of him like a weapon. The massive, shadowy form of the *thing* was getting closer, so close he was starting to work it out in his mind's skeptical eye.

Two simultaneous bolts of lightning laced the sky in a web of light. The lake was awash in visibility. So was Matthew. So was...

"Uktena..."

The serpent's head alone was huge, large enough to swallow Matthew *and* his car whole, if it felt so inclined. Its yellow eyes were taller and wider than he, and behind them sprouted mighty antlers like he had seen many times on grazing elk. The horns twisted up into the sky, shadowed by the blinding glow of the stone embedded in the silvery scales of the great serpent's forehead. Everything, it seemed, was cast into darkness by the intensity of that central light, it was Ulun'suti, he realized, just like the one he held in his palm.

For a moment, they regarded each other. He got the sense that it expected something from him—that it was waiting. But he did not know what it could want, and all he felt from looking into its huge, golden eyes was fear, tightening his chest and seizing his muscle. He could scarcely imagine how his ancestors had confronted such a beast, let alone slain one for the light in its crown.

The Uktena was the first to move. Its massive coils churned and twisted, stirring huge waves as it began to raise its head back up into the sky, watching him with the corner of one brilliant eye. The entire lake seemed to rock as its serpentine body thrashed beneath the surface.

"Wena!" It bellowed, splitting open its jaws and coiling its head back as if preparing to strike. The cry crashed over him, making his knees wobble. "Wena!"

Matthew had no idea what it was saying, but the power of its wail shook him to the core. The Uktena was turning away, angrily tossing its head, brightening the dark sky with the light of its beacon. It couldn't leave, not yet. Matthew could barely think through his shock and terror, but he knew they weren't finished. He waved his own Ulun'suti in the air.

"Wait!" He called, gasping for breath. "Wait! Please! My name—my name is Matthew Kidwell. I think my great-grandfather may have stolen this from your people." His hand shook as he held the stone above his head. A ripple passed through the serpent, the muscles of its body tensing and flexing as it paused and tilted its horned head down toward him. Matthew could barely hear the roar of the storm over the pounding of his heart in his ears, but he forced himself to continue, stammering for words and air. "I know this stone came from an Uktena, and I—I want to set things right. For my family, my sister. Please. It's not fair that either of us should suffer any longer for my ancestor's mistake. Let me make things ri—"

"Alewisdodi!"

Matthew was cut off as the Uktena bellowed and the breath was torn out of his lungs. He gasped and choked, collapsing to his knees. The tide-whetted stones of the shore tore open the fabric of his pants and cut into his skin, but he was only vaguely aware of the pain. Unwillingly, he turned his face away and tried to catch his breath as the serpent began to lower its massive head again, blinding him with the intensity of its Ulun'suti.

"Please . . ." he whispered, holding his own glowing stone between clasped hands that he held raised as if in prayer. "I don't know—" his voice broke with welling tears, "— I don't know what you want from me."

He shuddered and cried, thoughts racing, heart pounding. At any moment, he expected to be lifted into the air and swallowed whole by the horrible serpent. He composed farewells and prayers and apologies in his mind, awaiting his demise.

Nothing happened. Matthew remained kneeling on the rocky shore, hands raised in pleading piety, eyes squeezed shut from fear and despair.

A hot breeze tickled his skin and ruffled his rain-soaked hair. He flinched and shuddered, trying to ignore it, knowing it was not the night wind. The heat grew closer and stronger, forcing him to open his eyes and brush away rain and tears so that he could look into its source—the slightly-parted jaws of the Uktena. Its snout was so close that he could reach out and touch its smooth scales; the glow of its beacon blotted out everything except the face of the antlered serpent, its exhalations washing him in warmth.

Matthew knew he should still be afraid—he was closer to imminent death now than he had been while stranded in the Ouachitas as a child. But while tears of shock and confusion rolled down his face, he felt himself drained of his terror. There was something in the serpent's eyes, something intelligent. He saw no hostility—only caution, and perhaps even fear of its own.

"Of course . . ." he whispered to himself, neck craned back as he and the Uktena regarded each other at the shore where their worlds collided. "You can't . . . you can't understand me, either." The Uktena began to pull away when he spoke, but he desperately waved his hand, trying to signal that it was safe. It paused.

The realization that the Uktena could not understand him banished the last of his maddening fear. Its behavior made sense. All it knew was that a stranger had come, shouting in a harsh language, waving and clutching the remnants of what had once been another of its kind. The last member of his family to stand where Matthew stood had not come to help the Uktena. He had slain one.

Thunder boomed, and in the roaring of the sky, he heard his grandfather's ailing breaths, begging Matthew to set things right. The Ulun'suti had once brought wealth and good fortune, but it had come at a bloody price. The Kidwells owed a great debt, one they would continue to pay until the balance was squared. He only hoped that his offering would be good enough—that *he* was good enough.

Matthew looked up into the eyes of the Uktena, so vast in size and depth. It watched him, too.

"I'm sorry," he whispered, both to the spirit that his family had wronged, and to his own family, whose ways, language, and history he had neglected.

The storm-wrought waves lapped at his fingers as he tremblingly held the Ulun'suti at the edge of the water. He relaxed his grasp, realizing that it had been his own fear preventing him from casting it away. A part of him still wanted to cling to it, this remnant of his family's legacy. But he knew he couldn't. It wasn't his to keep.

Matthew breathed deeply and let go.

The stone rolled out of his palms and into the embrace of the water. When the waves receded, the Ulun'suti was pulled out with the current, drifting farther and farther away. Its light dimmed and churned beneath the crashing surf, and Matthew watched it for as long as he could, until the soft glow of his family's curse was swallowed to the depths of Lake Superior, from which few things ever resurfaced. The rain rolled down his skin, melting away an armor of grief he had not even known he was carrying.

The Uktena, too, was watching the jewel tumble beneath the surface. Far beyond the shore, Matthew glimpsed pinpricks of light flickering against the backdrop of the storm. The horned serpent turned toward this glowing haze. More Uktena, Matthew knew, coming to welcome their lost family home. He looked up at the great snake, the beacon between its eyes pushing away the night, at the way it yearningly twisted itself toward the horizon. Matthew yearned for his family, too, more than he ever had.

"Awanisgi," he said, the only word he remembered from his grandfather's stories, the one with which they always ended. "I am done."

"Awanisgi," answered the Uktena, its voice brushing over him like a soft wind rather than a booming thunder. Then it dove its horned head back into the water, illuminating the lake from beneath. The light left as it had arrived—streaking beneath the waves while the storm crashed and bellowed. The dancing beacons in the distance faded out of sight, as did the serpent with which Matthew had briefly spoken. It was as if nothing had ever been there at all. Maybe it hadn't.

Matthew shakily rose to his feet. Lightning flashed before his eyes and washed the world in silver before everything plunged back into darkness. Hastily, he fumbled for the flashlight, holding it in a trembling grasp. Though it speared through the night, it seemed permanently dimmer now; the light of the Ulun'suti had been a purer glow than any he had known before and might ever know again.

He turned his back on Lake Superior. The rain pelted him from behind, pushing him forward, back through the trees and back to his home. When he climbed up the slick, rocky shore, he felt a steadiness he'd not known since the Ouachitas, as if he'd found his balance again after all of these years.

The water fell away behind him. The forest was peacefully quiet but for the rustle of the leaves in the wind. He knew where to go, not only through the trees but also in the world, the only place he *could* go, now that he had let go of the past. *Forward*.

Awanisgi.

A'LIYA SPINNER

A'liya Spinner (he/him & she/her) is a non-binary activist, author, and aspiring paleogeneticist. She is a proud justice educator and learner in her local and online communities, and her creative works have been published in various locations. Most importantly, his favorite dinosaur is the Allosaurus fragilis. Talk about magpies, dinos, and queerness with him on her Twitter.

 twitter.com/cladist_magpie

LEAVE NOTHING TO CHANCE

CHANCE

ANNA ZIEGELHOF

Trigger Warning: Blood and death

Outside the castle there are creatures with claws and scales and teeth. Outside the castle a war rages. But inside the castle, everything is caused by the inhabitant of the castle.

The history of the world since the inhabitant moved into the castle:

—We say 'moved into' not 'fled into' because the outside is not permitted to cause.

Day One: the arrival

—We say 'Day' because the time that has passed after the inhabitant of the castle moved into the castle is indefinite. Nothing happened that would require the exact recording of time.

Day One was spent breathing and resting in a sheltered corner of the great hall. The most sheltered corner that a room called a hall could provide was the place furthest under the grand staircase where a just-grown human body just-so fit. Day One was spent in that shelter, resting and thinking.

—We say 'thinking', because we do not say 'worrying' when we mean the thorough analysis of all conceivable past causes and future outcomes of chains of events beyond our control.

In the evening

—We say 'evening' and mean the end of a timespan.

of Day One, the inhabitant of the castle formulated a plan. Day One was a long Day, and the evening of Day One was one of great hunger and thirst. A plan was made to leave the shelter to look for sustenance.

Day Two: the castle provides; first room

On Day Two the inhabitant of the castle added the first room.

—We say 'room' and mean an area in the castle explored on a given Day. The first rule was not formulated until Day Three. How do we know what a word like 'room' meant in a time before the formulation of the rules? We apply knowledge from the time after the formulation of the rules and remind ourselves that a word used before Day Three might mean something less well-defined. We accept this uncertainty. It is exempt from the rules.

The room of the second Day provided the inhabitant with food and drink. He found a pantry and a kitchen in the first room. After he had nourished himself in the kitchen, he explored a small chamber adjacent to it. In this adjacent chamber, he found a door. Bravely, he opened the door, but he could not bear the terror of what he saw behind it. He closed the door. He barricaded the door with a table. The chamber adjacent to the kitchen was declared off-limits.

—We accept this uncertainty. It is exempt from the rules.

The inhabitant of the castle shrank back into his shelter and sat shivering for the remainder of Day Two.

Day Three: the formulation of the first rule

The morning

—We say 'morning' and mean the time immediately after waking.

of Day Three was spent thinking in the shelter. The inhabitant of the castle was afraid.

—We say 'afraid' and mean unable to move, barely able to breathe.

The inhabitant was afraid of the unknown and unpredictable that still resided inside the castle with him. He was not certain if there were others in the castle or whether others would return. He was not certain if there were creatures in the castle or whether creatures would come. He knew that he would have to set out into the castle to check. The prospect of setting out into the castle filled the inhabitant with dread, and dread gave rise to the first rule:

Every Day I Must Expand The Castle By One Room.

Except on Day Three. Day Three was a Day set aside for thinking.

Making exploration a commandment was the only way to regain a feeling of safety and to defeat the feeling of dread caused by uncertainty.

—*We say 'feeling of safety' and mean the conviction that the world is understandable and predictable.*

Regaining a feeling of safety meant acquiring an understanding of, and the ability to predict, his environment, the castle.

Day Four: the second room and the second rule and the
third rule

The second room was an upwards expansion. Full of trepidation, the inhabitant acquired the second room, which took most of Day Four. In the evening of Day Four, he carried food found in the first room up the grand staircase into the second room and formulated the second rule:

Leave Nothing To Chance.

—*We say 'chance' and mean unpredictability or the absence of an obvious cause.*

After the inhabitant of the castle had settled into a shelter in the second room, which was a small chamber with bedding, he felt energized. Encouraged by the absence for four Days of events not caused by him, he formulated the third rule:

There Shall Be Nothing In My Castle Not Caused By Me.

Day Five: expansion

On Day Five, he expanded the castle by another room and returned to the second room in the evening.

Day Six: expansion

On Day Six, he expanded the castle by another room and returned to the second room in the evening.

Day Seven: the survey of the castle completed; the formulation of the rule regarding food

In the evening of Day Seven, the inhabitant of the castle noted that the castle had been surveyed in its entirety.

—*We say 'entirety' and mean those parts of the castle built above ground. The kitchen's antechamber is off-limits. The door found therein is beyond the physical and mental capacity of the inhabitant of the castle. We accept this uncertainty. It is exempt from the rules.*

The inhabitant of the castle rested and counted the remaining food. He concluded that food would soon become scarce and observed that the weather was not going to stay mild for much longer. In adherence to the second rule Leave

Nothing To Chance, he formulated the rule regarding food and the rule regarding fuel.

Day Eight: further rules regarding patrolling and rationing are formulated

On Day Eight, the inhabitant of the castle formulated the rules regarding daily patrols of the entirety of the castle and the daily counting of the food.

Day Nine: a peaceful time; rules regarding personal care; the windows are blackened

The inhabitant of the castle set to work to banish the outside after expounding the third rule, There Shall Be Nothing In My Castle Not Caused By Me.

—*We say 'in my castle not caused by me' but what if a sight from the outside causes a thought or dread or fear inside the castle?*

Doors were secured and windows were covered. The work left him exhausted and sooty, so the inhabitant of the castle added rules regarding the bathing of his body and the scheduling of the bathing of his body, accommodating the rules regarding daily patrols and the daily counting of the food.

The end of the peaceful time

The peaceful time came to an end when the inhabitant of the castle awoke one night.

—*We say 'night' and mean the hours during which the inhabitant habitually slept.*

A noise startled the inhabitant of the castle, breaking rule three, There Shall Be Nothing In My Castle Not Caused By Me. The sound had not been caused by the inhabitant. It was too regular to be caused by weather. It was too violent to be benevolent. It emanated from the kitchen's antechamber that was off-limits—specifically, from behind the door therein. In the darkness of his shelter in room two of the castle, the inhabitant of the castle expounded rule two, Leave Nothing To Chance:

—*'Leave Nothing To Chance.' Why do we follow this rule? To eradicate the unpredictable. 'Unpredictable' refers to the future. 'Chance' refers to the absence of an obvious cause. A cause lies in the past that brought us the present. Can we change the past? No. Can we change the future? Yes. Are we obligated to change the future to adhere to rule two, Leave Nothing To Chance? Yes.*

In the darkness of his shelter in room two of the castle, the inhabitant of the castle expounded rule three, There Shall Be Nothing In My Castle Not Caused By Me.

—*We say 'my castle' and mean 'the entirety' of the castle and mean those parts of the castle built above ground. But we say 'in my castle' and 'caused by me' so how about a sound from below the castle causing fear inside the castle? Is the inhabitant causing the violent scraping sound emanating from the cellar below the castle that is causing fear inside the castle? No. Can the violent scraping sound be permitted? No.*

Fortified by his expounding of the rules, the inhabitant of the castle fetched a weapon from room three. It was a fire poker. The inhabitant of the castle expounded the rules regarding fuel and found that an exemption from the rule against abuse of fuel was warranted. He lit a torch and descended from room two into room one and ventured into the kitchen and its forbidden antechamber.

A short meditation on rule three, There Shall Be Nothing In

My Castle Not Caused By Me fortified the inhabitant of the castle. He removed the barricading table. His hand came to rest on the doorknob. He would cause.

He caused the cellar's forbidden gate to swing open, causing surprise, causing an advantage. The inhabitant caused a roaring battle cry and lunged forward, causing his weapon, the fire poker, to enter the flesh of the intruder.

The intruder shrieked and fell forward into the kitchen's antechamber rather than back into the unknown abyss of the cellar. The intruder dragged their bleeding leg across the ancestral floor tiles. The intruder smudged the trail of blood with their pants.

—*We say 'nothing in my castle not caused by me' but do we mean 'death in my castle caused by me'?*

There was no time to expound whether death was allowed to be caused in the castle. The inhabitant of the castle backed away from the intruder.

"Fucking hell!"

The intruder, on the ancestral floor tiles, bleeding somewhat heavily through her pants, drew a gun. The inhabitant's torch was no match for the bright light the intruder had brought.

—*We say 'There shall be nothing in my castle not caused by me' and include 'my own death shall not be caused by me.'*

Thus, the fire poker was caused to clatter to the floor.

"Holy shit. You're just a kid."

The bright light stayed, but the gun was averted.

"I am the inhabitant of the castle."

He hadn't heard his own voice in a while. Fear made it wobble.

"The . . . castle . . ." she repeated and winced. She reached for the kitchen counter and pulled herself up. "You alone?"

"I surveyed the . . . castle. There is no other creature breathing its air."

"I see," she said and winced again. "I came in through this service tunnel or whatever. I was hoping to find shelter for the night. If you would grant it."

"Have you any food to trade?"

"I do," she said and winced a tear down her cheek. She groaned through her teeth. She hopped over to the sink. She unbuckled her pants. She dropped her pants. The inhabitant of the castle gasped.

"God, then just turn around, kid. I gotta clean this. What did you stab me with anyway?"

"Fire poker."

"Shit. If I die of some stupid infection, you're gonna have one big mess to clean up, dude."

"I'm sorry."

She scooped water onto her wound. She lowered her large pack to the floor and rummaged around in it. She applied salve and dressed the wound. She pulled up her pants.

"Are you a warrior in the war?"

She shut off the bright flashlight. By the flame of the torch, she was easier to see. She nodded.

"I guess that's what I am now. Guess that's what we all are now."

"I'm not. I'm only hiding."

The intruder was human. No claws. No scales. No fangs. She regarded him for a still moment.

"I need to change my story," the inhabitant of the castle said.

"Your story?"

The inhabitant of the castle confirmed this.

"It's easier for me when I have a story. One moment, please."

The Friend's Tale

IN THE DAYS of the desperate war, a warrior sought shelter in the castle of the friend. There was kindness in the warrior's eyes and the gracious host assisted the injured warrior to the grand hall. A feast was prepared by the light and warmth of the great hearth where many a heroic song had been sung to generations past.

"How long have you been hiding in here?"

Day One, indefinite primordial time, Days Two to Eight and into the peaceful time and until the end of the peaceful time, that is, today.

"What's your name?"

Wiglaf—a friend to heroes and kings.

"After we feast, please proclaim the story of your journey, O Warrior."

The warrior's tale went thus:

On the first day, the monsters spilled across the hills into the valleys. The great rulers of the valleys were unprepared. Many humans were slaughtered. Many were torn away in claws and beaks, on scaly backs. Many fled, carrying what they could. The warrior's beloved parents were among the ones horridly slaughtered, but the warrior escaped and traveled across the lands in search of revenge.

Had she killed many?

She had killed many.

"Wanna see?"

From her satchel she brought forth a collection of trophies: scales and claws and long spiny teeth, sharp piercers that ripped human flesh to shreds and caused agony and death. Each severed claw was the size of her callused hand that had wielded her mighty weapon against the abominations. Each spiny tooth was the length of her forearm.

"So they're real."

The warrior's tales were true.

"I sort of hoped . . . my Mom used to say I have a vivid imagination . . . It's too much."

The friend of heroes and kings shed tears in the presence of the warrior. She brought her strong arms around the friend and offered the comfort and safety of her body's vicinity until the friend dried his tears.

The friend had seen the creatures. But the friend knew of his own tendency for exaggeration and fantastic ideation. However, the friend also knew that what he had seen was death, and there was no exaggeration of death. The friend thanked the warrior for providing her power and her bravery to the peoples of the land.

"I've been hiding in here. I'm such a coward."

Friend, the warrior intoned, you have committed a heroic deed tonight by sheltering me, a warrior. Friend, the warrior praised, you have succeeded in staying concealed and alive in this remote castle. Friend, the warrior pleaded, would you allow your great hall to serve as a secret gathering place for warriors from near and distant lands in exchange for food and fuel?

The friend to heroes and kings graciously permitted his great hall to serve as a gathering and resting place for warriors from near and distant lands in exchange for food and fuel.

The warrior bowed and thanked the friend for his generosity.

The feast ended, the great hearth's last embers scintillated in the drafty hall. The mighty warrior lent warmth to the friend's body. Before a heavy sleep overcame them, the friend sang the praises of his dear mother and repeated the story of her heroic fight against the creatures and the noble sacrifice of her life.

"I'm so sorry, Wiglaf."

"I'm scared."

"I know. Me too."

ANNA ZIEGELHOF

Anna is a writer of genre fiction based in Northern California, focused on creating hope-forward, compassion-forward science fiction and horror stories. Most recently, her stories have appeared in The Future Fire, in Short Edition, and on the Tales to Terrify podcast.

twitter.com/annawithaz

instagram.com/annawithaz

Astromancy at the End of the Universe

Isabel Huntoon

Tam kneels on his side of the tent, mouthing the words he's praying to his god. I wish I could hear him. The repetition of words in his low, calm voice would be comforting, even though I can't understand them.

I can't even remember who his god is. I didn't ask when he came to the observatory in Tebelbel with the final group of adventurers, seeking an ace and an astromage to lead them to the world-eater. It hadn't seemed important at the time.

When he stops and lies down, I turn my head. I have enough starlight left in me to see him in the dark. Every time I look at him, my eyes stray to his prayer beads, as blue as they were in the star-given vision from my childhood.

"What is your god the god of?" I ask.

I can almost hear the smile in Tam's voice. "I pray to the god of memory," he says.

"Memory," I whisper. What a god to worship, when so many worlds only live in memory now. "How is that supposed to help against the world-eater?"

"I can't remember," he confesses, so seriously that at first I only blink at him. Then he smiles wide, and I laugh a little. "But I'm sure it will, somehow. At the very least, I'll be able to heal the survivors."

I hum, and our tent goes quiet. Foolish to assume there will be survivors. No one survives the world-eater.

That night, I dream of a giant star, so bright with blue light it blinds me. Its name is unfamiliar to me, its song frantic in energy.

In the morning, my luminous cup is full to the brim with starlight, and I drink well. I don't know where it could have come from; it has been years since enough starlight fell to fill my cup even halfway. Even before we astromages at the observatory noticed the world-eater, it was stealing our stars.

The starlight burns down my throat and races through my

veins. The stars in my blood sing, and I see what I often see in star-visions: a blue-green plain through smoke and darkness that clouds the stars' view. This time, though, the stars have given me more: a glimpse of the world-eater, the writhing chaos of its tendrils, opening its vast mouth to eat a star so tiny it looks like a speck of dust.

I shudder.

I want to make a starlet to hold in my staff, long empty, but I resist. Cold though I am, I need to preserve all my starlight. It will not be long before the world-eater takes all that is left, and I will have only the gentle light of our twin suns to drink.

Dɪᴅ I make the right choice, seeking out the world-eater? I look around at this pieced-together party, the remnants of so many lost worlds, dread heavy in my stomach. I am guiding us to our certain deaths, to be devoured like everything else has been.

But the stars showed me what their light had seen, years ago, when I first drank a cup of starlight and saw beyond myself. A priest in un-dyed wool robes, blue prayer beads around his neck, stood before a huge void. Next to him, a person with star-lit eyes and tattoos like the ones that sting fresh on my skin.

When we first saw the world-eater, first learned of its approach, I understood what the stars had shown me. I would stand before the world-eater someday. I did not see the people I travel with now. Only the priest, and the back of his shaved head.

When we stop for the night, I set up my stove at the edge of our small camp. The party leaves me alone, which I'm grateful for. They may need me to navigate, but I am not one of them, something they make clear at all times.

Neither is Tam, it seems. He also sits outside the close circle of the others.

"Why did we decide to bring the priest again?" asks one of the war mages, voice carrying through the still air. He plays with fire, drawing it up into a spiraling column. He is younger than me, and I wonder if this will be his first real battle.

"All he does is pray and eat." This, from the off-world gunner, M'xo Cruz. She polishes her cannon nightly and carries it on her back. The atomic shot in her bag clatters together like marbles. I don't know which part of the galaxy she is from, where they compressed nuclear weapons into bullets. Whichever planet she came from, it's gone now.

"Don't need him, do we?" says Nikir. They cook for the rest of the party when we find something other than nootch to eat. I don't know what else they do, what weapon they'll use to fight the world-eater.

"For what? When we get to the world-eater, we either kill it or we die," M'xo says. "Not much use for a healer."

"I'm craving calamari," says the Inodax celestial archer, sitting with his many legs curled under him. Datiadra, he asked us to call him. Those of us who are human or human-mixed cannot say his real name. His holy bow requires three of his four arms to draw—I have seen the photon arrows punch through boulders.

Laughter. I hold my fingers over my stove and watch as the water comes to a boil.

"We can leave him behind at one of the swamp villages," someone suggests.

"No," I say. The word feels unfamiliar in my mouth. They look at me.

"No, what?" says the war mage.

"No, we're not leaving Tam," I say. I ignore how hard my

heart beats. I've never spoken up like this before. Not even for myself.

"And you're the one who gets to decide that, hmm?" Nikir says.

"If you want to make it through the Shroud Sea, I am." I don't look at the ground the way the knot in my stomach begs me to. I can feel the weight of all their eyes on me. "What harm is there in his presence?" I ask. "The world is ending; there's no point in cruelty and arrogance now."

M'xo squints at me. "You're here to navigate, astromage," she says, "not tell us what to do."

They stop talking about leaving Tam behind, though.

Tam looks at me across our stoves. I swallow and look away, all my resolve used up.

"Thank you," he says, quiet in the darkness.

"You need to be there," I say. It feels safer than the words I keep behind my teeth: that he is the only reason I am here. That I've come to enjoy his murmured prayers as much as our shared silence at night.

Tam tilts his head. "I will be," he says. We are silent for a moment before he speaks again. "I can remember that, at least."

I stare at him. Have the stars shown him his future, too? His prayer beads shine in the firelight.

"Would you like to see them?" Tam asks, fingering the beads. Startled, I meet his gaze. I nod slowly, and he slips them off his neck and hands them to me.

They're body-warm and smooth as worn wood. I run my fingers over them. There's a small gap, the perfect size for another bead.

"Are you missing one?" I ask. I don't remember seeing an empty spot when I joined the party.

"Yes," he says.

"Why? What happened to it?"

He shrugs, looks off into the darkness. "I can't remember."

I hand his beads back to him, frowning.

AT THE EDGE of the Shroud Sea, where the land grows soft and wet, we borrow a raft from a small village. The people there retain the pronounced webbing between the fingers that their ancestors once spliced into their genomes.

They don't ask us to pay for the raft. We are one of the last parties heading east to the looming world-eater in the futile hope of stopping it. We don't know what happened to the other parties. We only know that they have not returned, and the world-eater is still there, hanging in the sky above the Greater Eldawny Plains, resting from its long swim.

Did the other worlds try to fight it, this vast and unfathomable thing that threatens us? Or did they see the death of the universe on the horizon and give in?

The party climbs onto the raft and blindfolds themselves. A villager hands me the long pole I'll need to steer us over the sirens' pits. She looks at us all with something that is not despair, not exactly. It's closer to resignation.

The sirens look like human-sized thunderstorms to me. Tails dark and wispy, formless bodies crackling with light, they flit around the raft. That's because their magic doesn't work on me. If the others weren't blinded, they'd be charmed to their deaths by something I can't imagine. I wonder what Tam would see, then frown at my stupidity. It's not as if it matters, with him a priest and me uninterested. But I like the way his tea-brown eyes wrinkle at the edges when he smiles at me. I would like it if he smiled at me more often.

He is blindfolded, like the rest of them, leaving only me to pole the raft through the murky swamp water. The air is thick and humid, and breathing feels like drowning.

At least the water is smooth, the way clear. The dangers here lie beneath the water. The sirens watch me, but they have no way to harm me. Their only weapon is attraction, drawing the unwary under the water. There, the sirens' physical forms sit with mouths open, digestive pits waiting for anything to fall in.

I don't look down at the water. I do not want to see how many sets of armor or weapons sit undigested in those mouths. Some parties don't want to go through the effort of finding an ace, but the Shroud Sea is the only connection to the eastern continent. I'm sure the sirens see the world-eater as a good thing, feasting as they must be on heroes and adventurers leaving the safety of the western continent behind.

I wonder, for the thousandth time, if this is worth it. If we should all be at home instead, enjoying the time we have left before the inevitable.

A GENTLE SLOPE of blue-green grass, soft and smelling of flowers, greets us on the other side of the first sirens' pit. I tie the raft to the derelict dock and lead the party over the crest of the hill, one by one. There, I unblind them.

Disoriented, one begins to stumble toward the water before I can stop her, the last trails of siren magic drawing her in. Tam turns, reaching out an arm to stop her, but then he catches sight of a siren, too, and I am running down the hill, heart in my throat. I catch their arms, but they pull away. I reach up from behind them, block their eyes with my hands. They pause. She tries to pull away, but Tam grabs onto her arm and keeps her within my reach. With their eyes covered, they remember why they should not step into the brown water.

"Come back," I say. "Carefully, take a step back with me." I guide the two of them back to the top of the hill and turn them away from the setting sun.

I relax once the hill is between us and the sirens' pit. There, we set up camp. I will do this again and again over the coming weeks until we leave the Shroud Sea behind and reach the wide plains that once housed a people so ancient that only concrete and steel survives them.

I sit facing the swamp, my small stove obscuring it with light. Tam sits down across from me. I frown at him, the worry from before coming back.

"You shouldn't have gone after her," I say.

I hear the others chatting and laughing in a group behind me. No one has invited me to sit with them, not that I would want to. But I can't tell if it's because they already know I'll say no, or if it's because they resent having to rely on me for direction, for having to bring along a shy, boring astromage ace to the end of the world. "It was reckless. You could have died."

"Each of us could die at any moment, even at the best of times," he says. He folds his hands in his lap and stares at the fire. "That's no reason to stop trying to help."

"The sirens are my job," I say. "As if one person straying wasn't bad enough, to have you go off and nearly get lured in —" I cut myself off and look away. I said too much. Tam didn't ask for the burden of my feelings, my worry.

"Thank you for saving us," he says carefully, and I bite the inside of my cheek. "But I knew I would be fine. I remember seeing the world-eater myself, so I can't die before then."

I stare at him. He begins to pray, holding his beads and murmuring words in a language I never heard before he spoke them.

"You're not afraid you might change the future?" I ask. I am, constantly—torn between worrying that I'm altering the path the stars have shown me and feeling arrogant for thinking I could.

"No," he says, confident. "I wouldn't remember it if it wasn't the future anymore."

I've never been that confident about anything, even leaving the observatory to find this party, despite the stars having shown it.

My skin feels cold without starlight, and I shiver. Tam pats the grass next to him, beckoning me with his heavy, woolen outer robe held out so that we can share it. I stare at him and see a small fear in his face, in his wavering smile and shy eyes. I scoot around until I am close enough to wrap the free end of his robe around my shoulders.

"Thank you," I say. He nods, and I see it from the corner of my eye. "It's so cold without the fires in the sky." I whisper because it's stupid, an astromage children's saying. *The stars are fires in the sky, and they warm us just like the ones planet-side do.* It's not incorrect, but it sounds stupid and simple, and I feel my face heat in embarrassment.

But Tam tilts his head back to look at the empty sky and sighs. "What was your favorite constellation, before all this?"

"The Lantern and Moth," I whisper, trying to hide the tremor in my voice that happens anytime I think of the missing stars. A tear rolls down my cheek and drops onto my knee. Then I rearrange my limbs and bare the skin of my shoulder and back. I look away as Tam peers at the constellation in my skin. The ink was mixed with a drop of starlight, so the lines and dots glow white, hot to the touch. "The eye of the Moth, the star Aleta, sang at the same pitch as my soul and called me to the observatory in Tebelbel. The Lantern and Moth were the first stars I drank from, and their light formed my staff." I reach down to my side and touch the warm surface of my staff. It hasn't been of much use on this journey, now that so little starlight reaches me. "It's hard to remember what they looked like now."

"I'm sorry," he says, and I think he means it.

~

ONE MORNING, there is a star chart at the foot of my bedroll, and Tam looks away bashfully when I turn to him.

"It was just something I had on hand for navigation," he says. "I thought it might help you remember your constellation. I'm sorry I don't have a better memory for you."

I swallow around the thickness in my throat and nod, clutching the paper tight to my chest.

The Lantern and Moth aren't on it, but I stare at the chart often on our journey, drinking in the memories of stars lost to the world-eater. It's painful, but I would rather remember than forget.

~

THE WORLD-EATER RISES JUST above the horizon, like a great, coiled star-serpent, long tendrils wrapped around itself. Dread sits heavy in my stomach every time I see it, and now I can't avoid seeing it. I have been guiding us to it all this time.

The plains of Eldawny lie flat and unbroken before us. It was farmland once, spreading out like a carpet around the massive city that once stood at the far end of the plains. Now it is wild grasses up to our waists, and flowers, and Chobeia bees fuzzy and fat as my fist, buzzing and bumbling through the sweet air.

As we walk, wading through the sea of blue-green grass,

Tam plucks wildflowers and braids them together. I watch his broad hands as they move, and grasses sway before me in the wind.

When we stop for a rest, Tam comes to me with his hands behind his back. He tells me to close my eyes, and when I open them, he stands in front of me with a crown made of iridescent flowers.

"For you," he says, and smiles when I take it. "They remind me of your eyes."

I blink and touch the skin under one eye. When I am filled with starlight, they glow. I can't imagine they are glowing very brightly now, though. Still, I put the crown on my head. My hair is dirty and unwashed, tied back for practicality, but Tam smiles at me, and I feel like I'm drunk on starlight, giddy from the warmth in my chest. I laugh a little, and the smile sticks on my face until we stop for the night.

By the time I notice the fog setting in, I can only see as far as my outstretched hand. Thick and white, it surrounds me in wet air. Panic pushes my heart into my throat, and I bite my lip to keep from screaming. We should have been prepared for this; traders on the satellites that used to orbit the planet could see the fog drifting over Eldawny for days at a time. I swallow hard, but it doesn't clear the thickness from my throat.

I turn to where Tam was, right next to me as always. But he's gone, and a tiny sob forces itself out of me before I clamp down on my frightened tears. I focus on taking breaths, on the ground and grass beneath my feet. I reorient myself. The world-eater is in front of me. The weight of it pulls at me like gravity, like a star tugging at my mind.

I siphon off a small amount of the starlight in my blood,

pouring it into the open crescent at the top of my staff. The starlet it forms spins bright and hot above me. This is all I can do in the fog; there's no more starlight for me to drink and see with, none except the twin suns above me, who see nothing more than I do.

I walk for a long time, and nothing about the world around me changes. The wall of fog is impenetrable, and a creeping fear climbs up my feet and wraps itself around me. When the fog is blown away by the plains wind, I will be alone. None of the others will be able to find me, or I them.

Still, I see through my starlet, watch where its rays land, and look for the shape of another.

My light hits a tall shape, shrouded ghost-like in vapor.

I hear Tam's voice, softly praying in the fog. I sob out a breath and rush toward his voice. When I run into him, we grab onto each other.

"I found you," I say. "I thought I'd be alone forever in there, lost in the fog." I am babbling, relief setting free the tears I was holding back.

"We're alright," he says. I nod. "We're alright." He hugs me tight to his chest, and I clutch his robe in my fists. His heart beats against me, and we are alive, together. "I knew you would find me," he says.

I press my face into his shoulder and laugh. "How could you possibly know that?" I ask.

"I remember it," he says. The ridges of his prayer beads press against my collar bone. I wonder how much of the future Tam can remember and how much of his confidence is pure faith.

"Do you remember if we find the others soon?" I ask. I am already searching for them with my staff, but my starlet is weak, and I'm wary of giving too much more light to it.

Tam hums and fingers his prayer beads. "Yes," he says.

"They'll reach the world-eater with us." I hold his other hand tightly.

Starlight bathes the skin of my face, and I tilt my head up to the suns to take it all in. I open my eyes. They shouldn't be able to give me this much light all at once, but I'm not going to question my good fortune. I pour some of it into my staff, and my starlet grows.

Tam and I set up our tiny camp with my starlet overhead, and in the morning, I can see other tents just at the edge of my view through the fog. I count them, hope and relief bubbling higher with each one.

Somehow, Tam's memories of success always come to be. Is that because of his god? The god of memory giving its last believer all it has? Do our suns shine brighter on me for the same reason, the last stars giving their all for one tiny astro-mage on the edge? I feel their light sink into my skin and warm me.

When the rest of us run out of good things to hold onto, Tam keeps a death grip on his god, on the prayer beads he keeps shiny and dry around his neck. Some small, envious part of me wishes he would give it up. How can he possibly believe it will help, even now?

A greater part of me wishes I still had something to hold onto. I used to have the stars—cool nights in Tebelbel spent wrapped in blankets with a pot of tea, watching them through the observatory telescope. Since the world-eater came, I see nothing but black in the sky, and it feels like someone has stolen the light from inside me.

I don't have faith in any gods. We haven't been saved, and

so many of them have vanished. Maybe even the gods are food for the world-eater.

But I do have faith in Tam. Tam the thoughtful, the kind, the persistent. Tam the hopeful, the giving. If there is one thing I believe, it is that Tam will continue to be those things until the end of the world or die trying.

Maybe what I want to hold onto is Tam. Maybe the good I'm fighting for is him and the way he makes me laugh, even at the end of the universe.

And, since the world is ending, and all my little fears seem ridiculous beside it, I tell him that.

"I can't give you any more than what we have now," he says, hesitant.

I shake my head. "I'm not asking for anything you can't give." Tam breathes out, and I sit back on my heels. "I don't want any more than this," I add.

Tam smiles, with teeth, and a little flame ignites in my chest.

"I remember," he says.

I look away, shy. A sudden, small hope makes me smile back. I have to laugh at the absurdity: I am happy on my way to the death of the universe. We move our bedrolls close together at night, and when we wake, I can see flecks of gold in Tam's eyes.

THE WORLD-EATER IS FINALLY STIRRING, filling the sky with its churning mass of limbs as we approach the center of it from below. I don't know how long it has been since we set out; each day passed out of remembrance as soon as it happened. This is my only future. I will not come back. I've known it from the start. The stars saw me standing here on this blue-green plain, among pitted, crumbling concrete ruins, with the world-eater right above me.

And then there is nothing, what once may have been my future—devoured already, yet to be devoured, being devoured now.

We will either kill the world-eater, or we'll die here.

The creature in the sky unfurls into something so massive I can hardly understand it. The party stills with sudden, hopeless fear. What can we, specks of dust to the world-eater, do against it?

Tam stands beside me, holding his prayer beads tight and whispering a prayer, low and fast.

"I remember you," he says, meeting my eyes. "I remember the way you glow. I know you'll be able to do it." I stare at him. My role is done. I guided the party here. The only other thing I can do is make a small light against the darkness.

The others do the only thing they know: they fight. I watch, gripping my staff tight with both hands.

The young war-mage throws the flaming ruins of the city at the world-eater, but the burning missiles hit its body and bounce off. M'xo fires atomic shot after atomic shot They sink into the world-eater's flesh and explode, raining irradiated gore down upon us. It doesn't care at all. It grabs at the sky with its tendrils and eats, pulling everything in the world toward it. It rips up huge swaths of ground that disappear into its mouth like nothing.

One by one, the fighters destroy themselves trying to kill the world-eater. There is no going back. The war-mages burn up their blood for one last scrap of magic; the celestial archers exhaust themselves for one final shot, and then they fall or are snatched up by the world-eater. The grass smolders around us from the remnants of their explosions, their last gasps. I can barely think in the chaos. Through it all, Tam darts through the grass and rubble, kneeling over the fallen with prayers and healing hands.

And still, the world-eater eats. It sucks up the atmosphere, the air from my lungs, the heat from the sky, and it moves to cover the suns. It is inevitable, and there is nothing in the universe that can stop it.

All that is left is us, Tam and me, surrounded by the dead and dying, by rubble and ash. Those who could fight are dead or eaten. My guidance meant nothing. Tam's faith in me is wasted.

There is nothing but darkness above us.

Tam is bloodied and dirty, but he grabs my hand tight in his, and I remember why I am here. Why I refused to give in to the world-eater, inevitable or not. Why Tam did, too. Why together we stand alone before the vastness of it, the only ones between it and our world.

I remember why I chose to follow the stars to this point; why I couldn't let this thing consume all I hold close without at least trying to fight back.

I will not go quietly into non-existence. I will not give in, even when the world-eater sits so close its gravity is a force I have to fight against, clinging to Tam, who holds fast to a ruin. Not even when the suns' light is blocked by its massive form, and I am left in darkness. I am alive, with Tam, and I will die before I give that up. If nothing else, I will not make myself an easy meal.

There is fear, so thick it chokes me, but in spite of it, I will not give up. I squeeze Tam's hand.

"You're so bright," he whispers. In this new darkness, this void of light, the starlight I have been saving up glows from within me, like an ember in a dying fire.

I look up at Tam. He is gray with sweat-stuck dust, not smiling anymore.

"Tam," I say. The world is still around us. Like the eye of a storm, chaos surrounds but does not touch us. "Can you ask the god of memory for a favor?"

Tam looks back at me and nods. "Anything."

"I need starlight." I close my eyes against tears. "Memories of the stars long gone. I can't see their light anymore, not even in my dreams."

Tam frowns like he's trying to remember something from years ago. He touches his prayer beads, and his eyes widen. He pulls the beads from his neck and drapes them around me. He prays, the familiar yet foreign words filling my head.

I see stars, the night sky brilliant with them, like a dark canvas splattered with white paint and swirls of color, as galaxies and gas clouds burn bright. These memories are ancient; the sky was darker than this by the time I was born, so many stars already devoured by the world-eater. I imagine drinking in this light until I am full to the brim. What I would see if I drank this much starlight, I can't imagine. I might burst from it.

I can almost feel the remembered light wash over me, sinking into my skin. How powerful astromancy must have been when the stars were so thick you could hardly see the space between them. When I look down, the prayer beads are gone, leaving just the empty string. Now when I listen to Tam's prayer, I understand it. He's not praying, he's reciting the names of the stars whose memory-light shines in my blood. One after another, he names them, and I know where each star was born, when they died, the elements they burned for this light.

I let go of Tam's hand. He was all that held me down, pulled me back from the gravity of the world-eater. Now, it draws me up.

The world-eater doesn't notice me, too busy glutting itself

on the sky. It is after our suns, the twins, orbiting so close they seem as one. It devours everything, gorging itself on whatever crosses its path, but it loves stars the most. Their light is so sweet, their energy so scorching.

Remembered starlight is almost as good as real, and when I pour all that is inside of me into my staff, it glows just as bright. I can't hold any back, or it might not be enough; even the Lantern and Moth on my skin go dark.

Every drop of light I have pools in the open crescent of my staff and compresses, and the starlet that it makes is the most luminous thing I've ever seen this close. It whites out my vision, burns my skin, and weighs down my staff so much I almost drop it.

But I keep hold and strike forward, releasing the starlet at the top of the arc. It soars toward the world-eater's thrashing tendrils, and the world-eater lunges for it, massive mouth wide open and grasping. It swallows my little star whole, and, along with it, its own tendrils.

It's the beginning of the end—the world-eater won't stop eating, even though it's consuming itself. It folds and stretches so it can devour more of its long, smooth body, all of it disappearing into the black hole of its mouth.

It eats until it no longer has a mouth, then collapses in on itself, into nothing.

And then it is gone.

I fall to the ground. Something crunches in a way that sounds painful, but I can't feel anything. My skin is empty and freezing. Now all the stars are gone, even the last remnants of their light absorbed.

There is fire somewhere nearby, an orange glow and heat. The smoking grass smells like lavender sugar and woodsmoke. I remember sitting at the top of a steep hill outside Tebelbel, the glow from my campfire tiny compared to the brilliance above me. I counted the stars in the Lantern and Moth and listened as they sang to me.

Tam holds me carefully. He is crying, but his lips form a smile I never thought I'd see again.

"I remembered you winning," he says. "There are so many memories I couldn't fit into this body, but the sight of you, standing bright against the darkness, I never let go of it."

"I'm cold," I say, as I shiver uncontrollably in his arms. "Tell me the names of the stars again."

Tam repeats his prayer, lingering on each name. They feel like matches struck near my skin, tiny bursts of warmth that barely touch me.

"Priests don't have prayer beads made of stars," I say. Tam shakes his head. Smiles at me.

"No," he says.

"What's the name of the god of memory?" I ask, teeth clicking together as I shake.

"Tam," he says.

In the still, starless night, I laugh. It turns into a sob that makes my lungs ache.

Tam sets me down on a clear patch of ground. My back is cushioned by ashes and grass. He looks at me, and the tears gathering in his eyes are the only stars I have to care about anymore. Sweat and blood and dust mix into filth on my skin, but he ignores it to press his lips to my forehead.

"I also remember you living," he says. "I'm certain of it."

I laugh again, but this time it gets caught with smoke in my lungs, and I cough fire. "I love you," I say. Tam kisses my forehead again, and I can feel unsaid words smashing against his lips from the inside.

"Tell me again once I've saved your life," he says.

He whispers the stars over me as he works, and I listen until my consciousness fades. The sound follows me into darkness, colors my dreams in pink and gold. I have a memory of waiting in a nebula and witnessing the birth of a star, the coalescence of dust and gas into light and heat.

IT IS day when I open my eyes. The sunlight hits my cold skin with a cleansing warmth. I bask in it. If this is the last thing I feel before I die, it will be enough. To know that the world-eater is gone, that there is something left, is all I need.

I muster all my energy to turn my head and see Tam asleep beside me. I slowly inch my hand toward his. When our fingers touch, he wakes, and we smile at each other in a field of death, under a sky with only two stars in it.

When Tam can stand again, he will carry me to a village at the end of the universe, and the people there will set out my luminous cup to catch what starlight is left for me. I will lie in a comfortable bed until I am warm again, and then I will walk outside into the sunlight. I will see a child picking flowers, a trail of Chobeia bees following behind. Tam will kiss my hand and pull me along behind him through tall grass, and we will be alive together, for whatever time is left to us.

ISABEL HUNTOON

Isabel is a new, not-traditionally-published author of speculative fiction. She graduated university with a degree in English-Creative Writing, and now is writing the kind of stories she wishes young Isabel could have read. Her greatest goal for her work is to remind readers that even one person can have a dramatic impact on the world, and that choosing kindness can be a radical act.

 twitter.com/isabel_huntoon

A BILLION PAPER STARS

A. J. VAN BELLE

As we left the wrecked city behind, the planet's atmosphere curved below us, a hazy blue arc in the main deck's big window. I walked over to stand next to Sergeant Roe, who gazed out at the planet shrinking in our wake. The chrome-and-gray lines here inside the military spaceship were hyper-sharp, too crisp and flawless to be real. The only thing real was that receding planet. The one with the city of ash and the rain of paper stars and the bodies without faces.

The deck remained quiet save for the soft hum of our life support system. The rest of the crew must be in the rec room or in their sleeping tubes. The smells of disinfectant and ozone stung my nostrils. No footsteps crossed the charcoal-gray floor, which shone with a high polish, empty and cold. There was no sound from Roe. No movement. Not even the sound of breath. But the silence held no hostility.

"I'm sorry," I said. "About that sample." I didn't know why I was begging Roe's forgiveness. He wasn't in command of this mission.

He replied with a nod that, somehow, felt like absolution. "This kind of mission sucks. No two ways about it. But we have a duty to identify the bodies so we can tell surviving family members their loved ones are deceased."

Since he didn't seem to judge my actions, I gathered the courage to ask about his. "What were you talking about? On that call to the base on Pheres?"

"Yeah, I know you heard that." He didn't look at me as he spoke. "Nothing."

I waited, but he offered nothing more. Kellyn9 retreated farther, a blue sphere in a void lit by an infinity of 14-billion-year-old paper lanterns.

Maybe I could lend Roe an ear, do someone some good after all. "Whatever it was—" I began.

He cut me off. "It was nothing." No animosity there, but no room for discussion. "Anyway, I took a look in the system and found the shipboard computer's autosave of the first run of sample 324D, the original results you deleted. I looked at the ID on the subject."

My vision grayed around the edges and everything seemed unreal, far away. I half-fell back a step.

"It's okay," he said. "I won't tell anyone. I get why you did it. It's hard to lose someone. Also hard to break bad news."

I had nothing to say to that. He knew. And he didn't judge me for it. Before I could come up with a response, he crossed the deck with silent strides and disappeared into the hallway.

Alone at the window, I watched until Kellyn9 disappeared. For a long time, I stared at the field of blackness dotted with distant fireballs. I tried not to blink, because when I did, I could still see the dust from decomposing bodies floating on the air and the layer of ash over the corpses like hot snow.

EARLIER

I am asleep and safe.

Surrounded by my cozy comforter.

And stuffed animals.

And my sister.

My sister is shaking my foot.

Stop. I want to stay in this cloud.

I opened my eyes to the blurry image of an arm reaching into my sleeping cubby, a hand jostling my leg.

"Stop! I'm awake."

"You slept through the wakeup call, my friend," Ryan said. Ryan Amand, my fellow tech specialist on this mission. "We're out the door in five minutes." He disappeared, footsteps retreated down the hall. I didn't want to be alone, not for a second on this lost planet.

I caught up to the rest of the cleanup crew and we headed outside into what should have been a beautiful, if sweltering, morning. Under a pearly sky, back we went into the city of the dead, piles of rubble still smoking, streets cracked where every dream of every denizen fell through.

I looked over my shoulder at the ship, nestled in the grass outside the city like a giant insect that belonged there, part of the wildlife. Looked at my feet as we followed a new route. New alley. New bodies.

I blinked too long, walking blind. The sky rained grim ash. But when I opened my eyes, the gray rain was gone, and it was only in my brain that the shadows fell from sky to shattered pavement. I staggered and someone grabbed my arm. "You okay?"

I covered my eyes with a hand. "Yeah. Just tripped." *No. I can't see what's in front of me. I only see hellfire.* I couldn't tell anyone. It would sound like attention seeking instead of a hallucination or whatever it was.

We split up, as before. I checked the map on my tablet and went to the first body down my private alley, the one where I alone would take samples this day. I knelt by the ruins of what was once an adult or a child and pulled out a sterile swab and unsealed a tube and told myself this was not a human being. This was a subject, a part of the job. Could be an ant or a leaf or a stone or . . . or a caterpillar.

Kids in the neighborhood where I grew up used to play with the caterpillars when they were thick on the trees in summer. Pluck them from twigs and put them in buckets. Step on them and smear the brightly-colored goo of their innards over the pavement.

These were not humans. They were not even caterpillars.

In the darkness of my mind, I put myself in a very small box. Where no one could hear me and no one could see me. The only answer was to not *be* anymore. I was not a person. I was not a thing. I was not. I was erased.

A thing that was erased.

Curls of lingering ash blew through the alley. They'd have been at waist height except I was on my knees. Maskless due to the heat, I inhaled. Choked. Coughed.

Hot smoke in my lungs. The smell of burning herbs or burning flesh. The smell of crumbling plaster.

The kids used to grind plaster to a pile of powder on the pavement and feed it to the caterpillars. Why? Why would anyone feed plaster dust to caterpillars? What good does an insect's suffering do for anyone?

I sealed the collected sample, replaced it in my kit, and moved on to the next body. Knelt again. Pulled a new sample tube and swab from the kit.

A place of shells, the same on the outside, all ash. All the features wiped to a uniform smear, everything that made them people gone.

Maybe none of us are individuals, really. Maybe that's an illusion. Maybe the whim of an upturned nose or a freckle is all that separates us from void.

I gave up because the kit felt too heavy in my hand, and I stretched out on the grease-smeared pavement within arm's reach of the corpse. Flung an arm over my face and hid my eyes in the crook of my arm.

Another thing they used to do in my hometown: fold stars from cream-colored paper and shower them from the trees. It was a funeral thing, a tradition going back for decades, kids climbing trees and making a warm snow of paper over a funeral procession. Crisp corners. All kinds of stars, four, five, six points. Some no bigger than a beetle, others as wide as my palm. I could feel them now. See them with my eyes closed. They were here, falling on me. I'd never seen them from this angle. I must be the person who died. A thousand of them, for a thousand mourners.

I pulled my arm away from my face and blinked at soft gray-blue brightness, a sky obscured by the paper stars.

"Specialist Hartley!" At the sound of the voice from the end of the alley, I drew in a painful breath and remembered where I was. Hallucination, dream, whatever that was, it was better than this hellhole.

"Specialist Hartley!" Sergeant Roe repeated. "You dead or just taking a nap?"

I dragged myself upright. "Very funny."

Roe approached. *No. Go away.* He stopped a few meters from me. "Seriously, everything okay here?"

"Yeah. It's just . . ." I let the sentence fall away, hoping he would get it.

"You want advice?" he asked.

"No."

He snorted and gave me a rare half-smile. "Good. 'Cause I got nothin'."

I sat on a hard metal chair in a small conference room. The ship's climate control blew cool air in my face, and my palms curled over the cold edges of the seat. Ryan crouched in front of me. My chest didn't want to expand with my breath. Sergeant Roe stood behind him, his arms crossed. Distant. So quiet he was like a hole in space instead of a presence.

"You've got to think back," Ryan said, voice soft. *He thinks I'm a child.* "We need you. No one is angry. You'll be helping us all if you just think back. The computer folder for the sequence data from 324D is empty, and there's no 324D tube in the freezer, and we *need to know* if something is missing. No one thinks you did it on purpose."

I couldn't look into Ryan's sympathetic eyes. I looked up at Roe instead, the face hard. Not angry, no. But not soft, not patronizing like Ryan's.

"Look," Roe said. "You checked in subject 324 as collected, but we have no sample and no data. If you checked it in by accident and still need to collect, fine, we collect. If you lost it, also fine, we collect again. But refusing to say anything about it . . . that looks bad."

Ryan ran a hand through his hair. "Maybe you put the tube in the wrong box in the freezer by accident? Is that possible?"

I looked past Ryan, past Roe, at the beige wall. Anything I said would lead them eventually to the identity of subject 324.

"It's about more than informing the families," Roe said. "There's a security reason we have to identify every single body in this city. The details are classified, but I'm authorized to tell you this much: there was a non-civilian member of this settlement, and we have to find that person's body."

Ryan twisted in his crouch and looked up at Roe. "Is that what the rush is about on this job?"

Roe didn't answer.

Ryan turned to me again. "Did you drop tube 324 or something? No big deal. It's like Sergeant Roe said. We just go get another sample from that subject."

The mention of *another sample* shook me out of the insanity that had gripped me for the past day or so. The walls of the little room wavered like a heat mirage. They would find out the truth one way or another. They would tell my mother who subject 324 was. I couldn't stop that from happening.

I leaned forward and looked down at the floor, tracing

every scuff mark with my eyes. *You tried*, something in me said. But there was never any point to trying. Did I always know that? *You're going to eat space bananas on board that ship of yours*, my mother said the last time I talked to her. She wouldn't want to know what I'd found. But I couldn't keep the knowledge from her, no more than I could stop the slow drift of ash through the hot breezes in those fractured streets.

"Yeah," I said. "I dropped it trying to put it into the extractor, and it spilled. Was gonna head back to the subject first thing tomorrow morning. Didn't want to put anybody out."

Roe gave me a solemn nod, and Ryan's shoulders relaxed. "Really? Is that all, buddy? Why didn't you just tell us?"

"I'm not supposed to drop samples," I mumbled. "I'm the molecular specialist. I'm supposed to be careful."

Ryan clapped me on the shoulder. "No worries. Everyone slips sometimes. Hey, it's only 22:00. I'll send someone out to that subject to get another sample tonight. No harm done."

Earlier

A shadow smudged the ceiling of my sleeping tube. There should be no shadow there, no stain, no mark at all. Only the smooth peach-colored paint. *Space paint,* my mother used to say if I mentioned something like the color of the walls on a spaceship. *What color is the space paint in your room? Are you going to eat space crepes when you're in flight, or are you stuck with those freeze-dried bars?*

No matter what, I couldn't get her to stop adding "space" in front of anything if she expected me to encounter it on board the ship. She seemed to think I lived a glamorous life because I worked for the galaxy's centralized civil and military governing organization. But she had no idea. I couldn't blame her, really.

She'd never left Santa Fe, let alone launched into space. Perhaps she watched old movies and pictured her offspring floating around in a marshmallow space suit with a bubble helmet, like an oversized baby with a white umbilical cord tethering me to my ship, the source of space crepes and all other nourishment.

I never told her the quarters on missions like this were the size of a coffin. That even when flat on my back I could reach the ceiling. Maybe that was the source of the mark: a hand-print. I might have done it in my sleep.

Space crepes. Space samples. Things that are lost in the void.

I knew what I would do. Knew it all night long, just wasn't honest with myself. Still wasn't honest with myself. *Maybe I'll just look. Maybe I'll do things by the books after all.*

But I knew I wouldn't.

The other sleeping tubes remained sealed when I stumbled into the hallway and made my way to the lab. Needed to run PCR on yesterday's samples anyway before getting out there to collect more from the bodies. Might as well get an early start. So I told myself.

I reached into the -20 freezer and pulled out the box with the samples collected the day before yesterday. The ones we ran last night. The answer I didn't want. The thing my mother was never going to hear about. Sample 324D. The 324th body sampled, run in well D of the machine. I pulled it out of the freezer storage box and dropped it into my uniform pocket. No one saw. No one would see. It would be as if it never happened.

After that, I took my time resetting the thermocycler while yesterday's samples thawed. When that was done, I lined up the sample tubes in the slots on the extractor. The machine would open the tubes, lyse the cells, and isolate the DNA. After that it would inject each sample into a separate well in the built-in thermocycler, which would then pass the amplified DNA to the sequencer. The whole process, from loading to screen readout, would take a little over two hours. While it ran, I would be out there with the rest of the crew, collecting more cells from more blistered bodies.

Why would someone bomb a peaceful settlement?

Why did I choose a dangerous military career while my sister chose to live in Marigold, an amicable soul in a region named for flowers? Why is the smart choice no guarantee of safety?

As I started the machine, Ryan walked in. "Time to go." He paced around the room. "Look, I know you don't want to. None of us do. But you can't hide in here."

"I didn't say anything." My time here lost in thought must have been longer than it seemed. "This shit takes time. I'm the only person on double duty here. Your tech expertise only comes into play if something on the ship breaks, but we're using mine every day."

"What's that in your hand? Come on. We've got to go."

What *was* that in my hand? I still held the empty 96-well plate, that was what. "I just need to autoclave this."

"How long does that take?"

"About 90 minutes."

"What? We don't have 90 minutes."

"Oh. Once I start the cycle, I mean. Putting it in takes about a minute."

"Well, do it and catch up. Not waiting for you." Ryan ducked out of the room.

I caught up to him and we exited the ship with everyone else. Across the grass. Into the ruined city. Tall weed stalks waved between fractured chunks of pavement, fast growers since the bombing. Yellow flowers topped them, clustery things, like bunches of grapes. Yellow pollen blew from them, a river of plant jizz in the air at chest height. "Plant jizz," I said aloud.

"That what you call it?" Ryan said. "Whatever."

"That's what . . . someone I knew back home called it." I didn't want to say her name.

Ryan stopped and ran fingers up and down one of the stems. The other crew members went on ahead and he didn't seem to notice. "The plants of Kellyn9 are self-pollinating. Every one of them."

"Okay. So they jizz on themselves. Masturbatory plants."

"Call it what you want. If you want to mammal-ize plants."

"Are they even really plants?" I asked. "If they're something that has nothing to do with Earth plants."

"They're close enough. There are only so many ways things can—"

"Will you two hurry up?" someone shouted, and we left the pollinating stalk and hustled to catch up to the group.

Once I turned down the alley assigned to me for the day, I made sure no one was looking and pulled sample 324D from my pocket. Dropped it to the dust-covered ground. Shoved it with my boot into a crack in the concrete and made sure it was out of sight in the darkness below street level.

*E*ARLIER

At the end of the work day, I was back with the smoke, with Ryan, behind a jagged half-wall of blast-stained brick as if it could give us some protection. The sample. The results I got in the morning. I didn't know what city she lived in, or even what planet, only the sector of space—until I saw the latest ID results: my sister's full name, along with her birth date and location, next to sample 324D. Micro-satellite domains don't lie. Not when everything else matches. I couldn't deny the fact that my sister's body was one of those in the bombed-out settlement. I'd scraped skin cells from her charred arm myself without recognizing her ash-covered face.

Everything tiny loomed huge, even the crumbling bits of brick on the ash-smeared pavement. *Who feeds plaster dust to caterpillars?* The blades of grass rising spindly from cracks in the pavement. What kind of creatures are we, to destroy so much? Our own mirror images, walking, talking, same two eyes two ears one nose one mouth . . . and we strike and hate and fear and break.

And bury in ash.

Scratches crisscrossed my forearms. Darkness crisscrossed the sky. No wait, that wasn't how this worked. Light fills darkness, not the other way around. Or is it?

Ryan sucked in a breath with a sound like steam hissing over rocks. Smoke curled from his nostrils. By itself, the military-approved, engineered-to-be-harmless calming chemical Nuttmek would be smokeless, but the herbs he added were fragrant on the air. He coughed, releasing more smoke into the gray evening, and I blinked and saw clouds of purple light because I didn't want to see the reality here.

"Didn't you say your sister lives somewhere in the Marigold sector?"

"No. Chartreuse." The lie came swifter than thought, bypassing reason the way a reflex bypasses the brain. The color names were nonsense. They should have given numbers to the sectors of space. Codes. Not colors. The regions couldn't even be shown in colors on a map because you can't project space onto a two-dimensional plane, so the color names were a stupid choice. If this area was a shade of yellow, it should have been canary. Canary in the coal mine of space, harbinger of humanity's implosion. Or was that what cleanup crews had said in ruins for time immemorial?

Someone shouted from far away, a voice bouncing off the brokenness of this city, signaling we were done for the day. Time to go back to the ship.

Ryan and I returned last. He disappeared to a rec room, but I headed through the deck to go to the lab. To be alone somewhere bigger than a coffin. To think. To be among the samples. Near the one that signaled a loss as big as a bombed-out city in my soul, the one that would also destroy someone else I loved.

Harsh words droned through the L-shaped main deck room, low and earnest. I didn't recognize the speaker until I rounded the turn and saw him. Sergeant Roe, but his voice was so rough and angry he sounded like a different person. He sat hunched at a video console, talking to a screen that showed a stranger in uniform.

"I don't care about protocol. You get her out of that cell and on an IV within ten minutes and send me a photo proving it or I will abandon my post and pull her out myself no matter who gets in my way." His voice thinned to a rasp. "If she dies, I'll see every single one of you convicted for manslaughter."

The stunned face on the screen blinked several times. Nodded. "Yes, sir. We'll take her to the infirmary."

Roe tapped the touchpad, ending the call without another word. He swiveled his chair to one side, curled in on himself with elbows on knees, and rested his forehead on both fists. His shoulders trembled with uneven breaths, and I thought he was crying until he lifted his face as if able to feel my stare. His eyes were dry. He didn't speak, but his expression said, *What are you looking at?*

I gave him a respectful nod. "Good evening."

Roe snorted.

"Everything okay?"

Roe's only response was a small tip of the head that said, *What the fuck do you think?* I left the room, went down the short, low-ceilinged hallway, and unlocked the lab.

EARLIER

I stumbled from corpse to corpse for ten hours. Sometimes with a mask on to filter debris from the air, other times barefaced because the mask was too hot, suffocating me.

After checking all the assigned cadavers off my list, I staggered to a wall on the outskirts of the city. Leaned against it, my back hunching with muscle cramps. I pressed my shoulder blades against the rough brick wall, sniffing, gasping. Why did my body have to betray me? I rubbed the heel of my hand over my upper lip, scrubbing away the snot. My eyes stayed dry. Too dry, stung by the ash in the desert of a trashed city. The storm clouds rolling by in high winds gave the impression the air was still full of ash from the bombing. But the bombing happened days ago. All was quiet in the surrounding space.

"It's better if you keep the mask on."

I jumped. Ryan squatted next to me against the partial wall. I hadn't heard him approach. "I couldn't," I told him. "It was a mess in there. Inside my mask, I mean." I wiped my nose again and my hand came away bloody. "You're not wearing yours."

Ryan rested his elbows on his knees and squinted at the gray-black sky. His brown hair flopped over his eyes and his brown skin shone with sweat in the greenish temp floodlights we'd set up. "Yeah. Felt like a caged animal in that thing."

And you think that's any better for me? I didn't have the strength to say the words aloud.

When I didn't say anything more, Ryan turned to look at me, and his eyes widened. "You okay, man?"

I wiped my nose and upper lip again. "I think it's just the bad air. Hard on the sinuses."

"It's time to knock off for the night anyway." Ryan fished in his supply pouch and pulled out a small object half the length of his palm, a spot of dull red in the gray surroundings. He handed it to me. "Here. Loaded it up already for ya. It's Nuttmek, but I added some mullein and skullcap so you can taste the smoke."

"They allow Nuttmek here?" I'd never tried the synthetic chemical, designed to be harmless for the lungs, but I understood it was forbidden to enlistees on duty. And when you were on a mission like this one, you were on duty 24/7.

Ryan snorted. "First time on cleanup, huh?" He pulled out an old-fashioned butane lighter and tossed it to me. I fumbled and dropped it despite how little distance was between us. "You're bleeding. Your reflexes are fucked up. And you've got goosebumps even though it's 40 Celsius out here. You, my friend, *need* a smoke."

I picked up the lighter, put the smooth red clay pipe between my lips, and tried to wake a flame. My thumb slipped uselessly over the metal wheel.

"Give me that." Ryan plucked the lighter back from my hand and held a yellow flame to the pipe's mouth. "Breathe. Or did ya forget how to do that, too?"

I snorted, and my laugh sprayed drops of blood on the pipe. I inhaled. The heat of the smoke spread through my lungs. Something you wouldn't feel with Nuttmek alone. I nodded in appreciation, holding my breath. "What do those other two things do?" I asked when I was ready to speak. "Something and skull something?"

"Mullein and skullcap," Ryan replied. He motioned for me

to take another drag. "They're herbs. Not really psychoactive, but they can help calm you down."

"How do you know all this shit?"

Ryan swiped a hand through the air in front of him as if revealing an imaginary marquee projected on the sky. "New Galaxy Herbs. That's my parents' business."

The mention of his parents made me wonder where my sister was. Somewhere in this sector, a cone of the inhabited galaxy named for a shade of yellow. As children, we used to watch funeral processions together and pretend the rains of paper stars were snow.

EARLIER

On the first day, smoke rose from cracked half-buildings, mingling with mist against a gray-green sky. I had a tablet clipped to my belt listing the samples I was supposed to take that day. A digital map showed where each corpse awaited me. The plastic filter mask bit into my nose and cheeks.

"This is my street," Ryan said, voice muffled, face already sweaty in the hot morning. "A piece of advice: don't think. About anything." He disappeared around a turn.

I checked the map and split off from the rest of the group to follow my own predetermined route. It took me down a narrow alley where bomb-blackened walls rose too close on either side of me. My breathing came rapidly. *Just the mask. Just the illusion of breathlessness.* That thought didn't help, so I pulled the mask down and let it hang around my neck. Coughed until my eyes teared and I saw the ruins through the film of damp as if through a wide-angle lens, making everything at once sharper and farther away.

Only a few meters to go before the first body, according to

the map. My heart beat hard and sharp. I stopped and looked behind me, sure something awful was following me. But there was nothing.

Of course not. Whoever devastated this peaceful city wouldn't be coming back. Or, if they did, our ship's sensors would pick up their approach with plenty of time for us to clear out. That logic didn't tame the feeling, though. A heavier layer of clouds rolled in, darkening the alley, and I felt like a little kid afraid of the dark. Except that there really was death in this city.

Everywhere you turned.

I got to the place where the map said our sensors picked up a body, but I didn't see anything. A trash bin taller than I was, bags of refuse spilling from it. The smell of rotting vegetables. Chunks of masonry strewn in my path, gray stone and a lump of gray—

Oh. *That* was the body. Covered in a layer of salt-and-pepper cinders, like burned-out charcoal. And small. A child.

My arms and legs shook, fighting conflicting urges to scoop the dead little one into my arms, as if I could comfort one already departed, and to run back the way I came, find somewhere to hide and pretend dead bodies existed only in stories.

I dropped to my knees beside the child's remains. They said not to move the bodies unless they were buried and we couldn't get a sample. Otherwise, leave them undisturbed and take a few skin cells for DNA sequencing.

But this was someone's kid, and a fallen piece of limestone obscured half their head. The features were burned away, leaving only a layer of gray soot where the face once was. All the same, out of respect, I should not leave the debris atop the dead. My fingers wandered, trembling over the sandstone fragment like spider legs. Something other than conscious thought animated my body. It didn't feel like me. I only watched. The edges of the stone bit into my fingertips, but I felt nothing as I tipped the masonry aside.

I snapped back into myself, chilled to the bone in the heat. Protected under the fallen rock, the other half of the child's face was intact. Skin slack and purpled with bruises, the one remaining eye half-open and blood red. Long hair the color of maple syrup. Someone's daughter. Someone's little sister.

Dust blew into my eyes. I stared a long time, losing minutes, floating somewhere just behind my body, until I roused enough to promise myself I would call my own sister as soon as this mission was done. She'd moved and I hadn't heard from her in a while. No bad blood between us, we were all just too busy.

The wind riffled the lifeless child's hair. Joints stiff, muscles locked, I forced myself to pull a sample tube and swab from my kit.

EARLIER

I sat in a cubicle in a corner of the ship's rec room, tablet on my lap, opening a star relay connection to Mom's tablet back on Earth. The low hum of laughter and the crack of billiard balls formed a backdrop of sound as my crew mates played pool nearby. Mom's soft face and gently worried eyes appeared on screen, with an adobe wall behind her and blue sky above. "There you are! I hope they're feeding you well on that spaceship."

I smiled. "Always, Mom. You're sitting outside. The weather's nice?"

She nodded. "It's cooled off enough to enjoy the courtyard. I've even planted some asters. But I haven't heard from your sister in a while. Have you?"

"Yes." It wasn't a lie. I'd heard from her more recently than Mom had, at any rate. Mom didn't need to know the message was a few weeks old and that I'd heard nothing since my sister's interplanetary move. "Let me pull up the recorded message she sent me." I touched the message icon so the recording would show up as a split screen for both me and Mom. My sister's face came to life against a shiny steel wall that could have belonged to any transport ship anywhere.

Mom put her chin in her hand and took on her thoughtful, listening look. The New Mexico sun warmed her gray-blonde hair.

"I'm on my way to my new home in the Marigold Sector!" my sister said in the recording, her eyes bright. "My place will be in a really pretty town. It's hot there but so nice. There are yellow wildflowers in the fields right next to the town. I won't tell you exactly where until after I settle in. I want it to be a surprise. You'll like it, though. I can't wait for you to come visit." She glanced away from the camera as someone said something to her in a muffled voice. My sister nodded at the person off camera, then turned back to the screen. To me. "I have to go now. I'll call you as soon as I get a free moment. When you're on leave, come see me and we'll explore." Her face vanished.

Mom in her peaceful desert courtyard filled my screen again. "Well, that sounds very nice," she said. "I can't wait to hear more about her new home planet. You'll have to visit *me*, too. Do that the next time you're on leave near Earth. You hear me?"

"Of course, Mom." Thinking of visiting her, of hugging her, I could almost smell the soft vanilla perfume she liked to wear. "It's been too long."

The lights in the rec room dimmed, and at the same

moment a loud clap of resin-on-resin came from the pool table.

"Time to turn in!" someone called out. "We'll be at Kellyn9 in a few hours, and we start early."

I peered over the cubicle wall and saw Ryan rolling the cue ball across the table by hand and sinking it in a corner pocket. "Aw, hell," he complained good-naturedly. "I just broke for Nine-ball."

"Sorry, Mom," I said. "I have to go. On ship's time, it's getting late. But I'll call you after the mission is finished."

"You do that," she said, and her warm smile looked like home under the hot desert sun. "You eat some space crepes in the morning to keep your strength up before you head out to work, okay? And if your sister calls you again, remind her she still has a mother over here who worries about her."

I told her I loved her, shut down the tablet, and headed toward my sleeping quarters. I didn't mind crawling into my coffin-sized tube—not knowing my sister was now in some cozy new home, that she was excited about it, and that she would invite me to visit as soon as she was settled in. And knowing my mother was out there sending us both her love across the vastness of space.

A. J. VAN BELLE

They write genre-bending fiction and work as a biology professor and molecular geneticist. When they're not writing stories or code, they explore the woods with their two dogs and invite their husband and teenage daughter to listen to the plot twists simmering in their brain. Their profession as a molecular biologist informs this story's use of DNA sequencing for victim identification.

ACKNOWLEDGMENTS

A huge thank you to all those who helped make this anthology a success. A very special thanks to Jennifer Flaig for organizing the submission and judging process for us. The anthology would not have happened without her help.

To our judges—who carefully read and agonized over each and every story—we appreciate the time and care you took. Much appreciation to our Editor in Residence Justine Manzano who assisted with dev editing and proofreading, and to Dakota Rayne and Sangy Crowe from Inked in Gray who provided editing and formatting. Our cover designer is Antoinette Van Sluytman, who did an amazing job illustrating the theme.

Most of all, thanks to those who submitted to our anthology! Writing is hard, but it's also a labor of love. Keep reaching for your dreams.

With Love,
All of us at WriteHive